THE
AMBROSE J. AND
VIVIAN T. SEAGRAVE

MUSEUM OF
20TH CENTURY
AMERICAN ART

THE AMBROSE J. AND VIVIAN T. SEAGRAVE MUSEUM OF 20TH CENTURY AMERICAN ART

A NOVEL

MATTHEW KIRKPATRICK

CINCINNATI 2019

Acre Books is made possible by the support of the Robert and Adele Schiff Foundation.

Printed in the United States of America
First Printing

Library of Congress Cataloging-in-Publication Data
Names: Kirkpatrick, Matthew, 1974– author.
Title: The Ambrose J. and Vivian T. Seagrave Museum of 20th century American Art / Matthew Kirkpatrick.
Description: First edition. | Cincinnati : Acre Books, 2019.
Identifiers: LCCN 2018061500 (print) | LCCN 2019002990 (ebook) | ISBN 978-1-946724-17-5 (ebook) | ISBN 978-1-946724-16-8 (softcover) | ISBN 1-946724-16-5 (softcover) | ISBN 1-946724-17-3 (ebook)
Classification: LCC PS3611.I764 (ebook) | LCC PS3611.I764 A83 2019 (print) | DDC 813/.6—dc23
LC record available at https://lccn.loc.gov/2018061500

Designed by Barbara Neely Bourgoyne

The press is based at the University of Cincinnati, Department of English and Comparative Literature, McMicken Hall, Room 248, PO Box 210069, Cincinnati, OH, 45221–0069.

Acre Books books may be purchased at a discount for educational use. For information please email business@acre-books.com.

for Matilda

THE AMBROSE J. AND VIVIAN T. SEAGRAVE MUSEUM OF 20TH CENTURY AMERICAN ART

Gaylord Kellogg
American, 1891–1937

Two Birds, Blue Ball, 1925
Feathers, oil on emery paper, mounted on plywood

Kellogg retreated from public life from 1925 until 1927, a period during which, some scholars argue, the artist produced his most important work. Kellogg's *Two Birds, Blue Ball* marks the beginning of this span and reinvigorated the public's interest as the artist shunned his usual subjects—arbors, crumbling fortresses, nude girls cast in fragmented light—in favor of animals, here entwined birds hovering over a smooth blue sphere. The presence of the blue orb, like an alien billiard ball in the otherwise pastoral scene, suggests a scar or a hole. The ball is so obviously out of place, and yet the birds pay it no heed. Note that the artist chose two female cardinals—the plainest birds—as his subjects. The work also represents one of the artist's first uses of collage, incorporating actual feathers collected by Kellogg on long early morning walks.

Clancy Scott Carter

American, 1922–2014

The Rabbit Surfaces, 1966

Oil on linen

The Rabbit Surfaces belongs to Carter's *Subterranean* series, which explores the landscape around Carter's boyhood home near the Allegheny National Forest in northern Pennsylvania. Created at a pivotal moment in the artist's transformation from surrealism to abstraction, *The Rabbit Surfaces* was his first large piece, executed by Carter fixing the linen to the floor of his studio so he could work around the entire painting. While the image of a rabbit emerging from a hole is suggested by shape and color, Carter's focus here was on the *process* of painting, on celebrating the potency of unstudied and impromptu action rather than the precision of representation.

Lorena Erickson
American, 1905–1995

Devil's Tower #3, 1970
Oil on canvas

After living in Wyoming for two years, Erickson returned to her childhood home of New Paltz, NY, but remained committed to the landscape of the American West, which she claimed represented the true spirit of her native country. In *Devil's Tower #3*, the dramatic intrusion of the stark monolith on the rolling plain literally overshadows the figures, on horseback, as they advance. Erickson believed that nature would ultimately triumph over the encroachment of humans, and here the enormous rock formation, seeming as if it is about to swallow the inconsequential explorers who approach it, symbolizes her conviction.

Harley Booth
American, 1901–2014

Ergodic Texture, 2000
Watercolor and pencil on paper

Subtle creases in the paper create troughs where the paint has collected like water might in valleys on a topographical map. The light touching the edges of each faint fold mimics the light that touched Booth's eyes as he stood in some dead field and was so bored by what he saw that he chose to paint something entirely different.

Mallory Claunch
American, 1949–

Second Helping, 1989
Plaster and acrylic paint on canvas

Second Helping is one of the last pieces by Claunch that might be considered a painting as, by 1991, the artist had transitioned to exclusively sculpting in plaster. The plaster objects extending from the surface of the canvas suggest the meal depicted is about to spill onto the floor, as if the canvas were too limiting to contain her vision.

Iris Babbitt

American, 1940–2007

The Water Cure, 1971

Latex house paint, gravel, plywood

The Water Cure uses artificial materials as a medium for the careful arrangement of gravel. Man-made substances not only anchor the natural material, but also highlight it, transforming the ordinary and overlooked (gravel) into the sublime (colorful gravel). The hue of the painted gravel, as well as its sinuous shape, evoke water, another paradox in the antithetical properties of liquid and stone. Babbitt's ghost sometimes dresses in a frockcoat, bow tie, and top hat like a nineteenth-century dandy and performs improvised plays in the attic. Though I know it is my Babbitt, it frightens me.

The painted stone evokes water.

She is unaccompanied this warm morning.

She remembers sitting on the edge of her bed in the gauzy dawn filtered through the sheer curtains, feeling the strength in her legs. She would poach an egg and go for a walk.

She would go for a walk and do her errands: write a few checks, drop them in the mailbox. She would withdraw money from the bank, leave a dress with the dry cleaner, stop at a friend's bakery to check in. A neglected pipe beneath the street had burst and flooded the shop's basement, had ruined equipment, boxes of paperwork, bags of flour and sugar. She would comfort her friend, standing with her before the still water in the musty basement, give her an envelope on her way out, just a little help.

What can be cured with water?

The museum was a curiosity in their small town. Rare sightings of the curator around town had turned him into a legend. On the few occasions when she'd seen him, the curator always looked to her like he wanted to be anywhere else; he always seemed to be lurking, shuffling into the shadows to avoid being spoken to.

She has been meaning to visit the museum for years. And now she was here. Something about the smell of the interior . . . something familiar.

A boy, maybe six, stands too close to the Babbitt with his hand jammed into his enormous mouth. He too is unaccompanied. She looks for a guard but sees no one, and when the boy removes his hand, saliva drips down his fingers in syrupy strands. He looks at the artwork, extends his fingers so the palm of his hand is parallel with the surface of the piece. He smiles and slowly moves his dripping palm closer.

She hears the lapping of the lake on the stony shore, hears the crying of gulls, the wind over water. She tries to remember the sky—a gray day, surely, because of the rain—but cannot imagine it. She can feel the wet gravel in her hands, sliding between her fingers, can see the way the current arranges the green strands of grass like hair on the thin band of rocky bank.

A sandhill crane swooping from the sky, gliding across the surface.

The boy stops, looks behind him. They lock eyes, and he is suddenly weeping, running away into the next gallery.

What she will do next: lunch in a café, the grocery store, a long walk home.

She steps closer to the Babbitt and looks at the gravel, the way the blue paint washes over the gray and taupe of the stone. She wonders if she feels something, if she can make herself feel something.

She tries to imagine the ghost of the artist performing a play in someone's attic, tries to imagine the loneliness of the reclusive curator, in love with a spirit.

She will be dead soon: perhaps today, perhaps in a year, maybe five. She wonders about her ethereal body, whether she will share the painful fate of the artist, damned to some attic.

Would that count as yet another life? Could she hang on after her corporeal self was gone? Perhaps she could haunt a happier place: a horse barn, a sunroom, a sailboat. She smiles at the comfort of ghosts.

Now a young man stands next to her. He is not dressed for the museum; he is wearing sneakers and pajama pants and carries a fringed bag slung from shoulder to hip. He smells a bit like Lysol and slinks around the painting, examining it from multiple angles. He squints and holds his hands together behind his back. He reads the card, pausing to look at some detail of the Babbitt, decoding it.

He releases his hands and rubs his chin with the tips of his fingers. With his phone, he takes a picture, then takes a step closer and snaps a photo of the gravel. He takes a photo of the card, looks at her, gestures toward the work, and nods as if to say, "I like this one."

"Yes," she says.

She took a bath the night before, drank a new kind of tea, and tried to read a book, a paperback thriller she'd found while cleaning out the spare closet. In it, two characters talk on a train.

The painted stone evokes water.

The painted stone does not evoke water, only gravel, wet with a boy's saliva.

What is missing is the gasping, the struggling against the current. What is missing is the murk and brown of real water, close and swallowed, how one can feel claustrophobic in so much space, submerged and helpless against the weight. This, she decides, is not water.

She remembers water.

Annette Morgan

American, 1925–2011

Wedding Day, 1967, 1968

Oil on beaver board

This now iconic image was inspired by Morgan's trip to her home state of Pennsylvania, where she witnessed a small-town wedding in which it seemed to the artist that every inhabitant of that place was a participant. "We watched the wedding procession wend through town like a parade, arriving at a little white church at the end of the street on the prettiest spring day," she said of the scene she re-created in *Wedding Day*. "I couldn't imagine how they were all going to fit in that church! Of course they didn't—they spilled out of the building and crowded around the doors and windows, all hoping to catch a glimpse of the ceremony. I wonder whatever happened to that couple!"

If Morgan were alive, I would tell her that the groom went to Vietnam the following year and never came back. His widow moved back in with her parents for a time and worked at the underwear factory with everybody else from her high school. Several years later, after giving up hope that her husband would ever return, she wed a man twenty years her senior—a gas station manager with wiry hair, a thick belly, a penis like a garden snake, and a suspicious laugh. He was kind to her, but he was not the love of her life, and the sadness of the loss of her first husband hung over their marriage. The two divorced in 1978, shortly after the birth of their only child, a son. Afflicted with a swollen heart, he required a series of brutal and archaic surgeries and died in 1983. In 1985, police killed her estranged second husband when he attempted to rob a bowling alley, and in 1986, one Sunday before coffee hour, she hanged herself in the church basement. Or none of that happened. I have no idea.

Compositionally, *Wedding Day, 1967*, is an achievement because of the sheer number of people rendered, the balance of so many figures, the details of their faces—one can see the joy in every eye and smile, even feel *as if we were there*, as if 1967 was nothing but the best year ever, everybody together, sharing in the beauty of the light and love of a perfect spring day.

Bernát Csillag
American, 1901–1965

Automatic Landscape, 1959
Oil on Masonite

Csillag is perhaps most famous for drowning in paint while working on an outdoor mural in Akron, Ohio. So unusual was his death that he enjoyed posthumous fame and an unprecedented demand for his trite abstract landscapes. *Automatic Landscape* showcases Csillag at his most humdrum: oblique shapes, spasmodic lines, and seemingly thoughtless splotches of color like spills.

Limited-edition paperweights inspired by *Automatic Landscape* are available in the gift shop.

Katrina Ho

American, 1955–1990

(Witch) Tree, 1980

Wallpaper, acrylic paint, shelf paper, etc., on plywood

Ho's interest in the "Witch Tree"—a 300-year-old (possibly older) *Thuja occidentalis* on the shore of Lake Superior—began as a girl, when she and her family would visit her paternal grandparents in Minnesota near the shore of the lake. She has described these visits as idyllic, though after her death, her brother explained that he and his sister suffered a childhood of sexual abuse at the hands of their father, so their trips to Minnesota "were idyllic, in a way, because the threat of our father was alleviated by the presence of his parents. Sometimes I wondered what they knew."

Here, in one of the first in a long series of paintings of the tree, the bark is rendered with textured floral wallpaper while the shimmering water of Lake Superior is painted over ordinary shelf paper. The depiction of this sacred tree with materials symbolic of domesticity suggests something below the surface—something seething beneath the bark, beneath the water, beneath the fleurs-de-lis of the fuzzy, mint-green wallpaper.

Artist Unknown

The Country Home, ~1930s

Dollhouse from the Kendall Seagrave Memorial Dollhouse Collection
Gift of the Ambrose J. and Vivian T. Seagrave Family Trust

Believed to have been commissioned for Kendall Seagrave by her parents for her fifth birthday, *The Country Home* is a stern Beaux-Arts country estate overlooking an expansive garden. The detailed reflecting pools and landscaping are all modeled after real gardens. Upon opening the back façade of the dollhouse via concealed hinges, one can gaze into the elegant rooms, through the windows, and out onto the prim vegetation beyond. Note the symmetry and details: the gilded pediments, the marble statuary, and the miniature paintings that adorn the grand hallway—all portraits of the Seagrave family's ancestors, painted by renowned miniature portraitist Gary Taylor.

She circles the house, examining the details of the fountains, the water so real and blue, the marble planters, the stone cherubim lining each side of the staircase leading down the hill from the house. The perfect boxwoods, pruned and verdant. The swimming pool surrounded by empty wicker chaises, a single clean towel folded neatly on each. On one of the side tables, a martini glass, a paperback book, an ashtray, a pair of sunglasses. The details are so perfect she can put herself there on a warm afternoon, reading, relaxing, waiting.

She hears a soft whine, like a bird, from above.

She can taste the last of the gin in the martini glass, stolen from whoever left it, smell the chlorine of the pool, feel the pattern of the wicker imprinting into her back.

The sun has always tired her; she looks into the house, cool even on the hottest day of summer, and thinks to retreat there despite what she can hear coming from inside: a door slamming, a man's voice, too loud, too sharp.

A noise from behind her like a slap; she turns, sees the young man in the pajama pants. He's dropped a notebook, scraps of paper scattered all around. Somebody calls to her from inside the house, a name she does not remember, but hers, nonetheless.

She leans to look inside. The façade is closed, but she is content to peer through the windows; the interior is illuminated from within, and she can see fragments of the ornate, miniature furniture, see the faces of the tiny portraits in the long central hall, dark and indistinct.

From the front of the house, the French doors open to the wind, and in the grand foyer three men in felt suits stand together, their arms frozen in wild gesticulation. From behind the tallest doll, a majestic miniature landscape in oil commands the room.

Something about the painting, something about the men arguing. The scene feels familiar, like a dream. The way one of the men's hands is raised, impossible to know if he is angry or exuberant. The landscape, a mountain lake surrounded by tall pines in winter. Something about the face of the man with his raised hands.

She remembers walking alone in the woods at the edge of a garden. She remembers hiding in the canopy of a pine tree, watching a man in a bird mask holding a champagne glass on the other side of the fountain.

He exhales; blue smoke emerges from the feathery edges of the mask. She cannot see his eyes. He is not a man in a mask at all, but a bird, enormous and oil-black, his eyes empty and colorless. He wheezes, coughs as if something is coming up. Choking, he extends his wings.

The young man is on the floor. He's gathered the papers, tucked them back into his notebook, but instead of standing, he seems content to sit with his legs crossed, one hand resting on each knee, his notebook before him. He stares away from her at one of the paintings on the wall, breathing deeply and deliberately.

The face of the man in the dollhouse reminds her suddenly of her husband, a decade dead. An image of him at the end of a party: a rare night when he'd had too much to drink. He'd recounted a story about the navy from when he was in Beirut. The story was one he told again and again during their life together, always changing details, refining it over the years into a ridiculous tale: a chase, a missing girl, a mistaken identity. She remembers feeling empty after their guests had left. Just some couple they had known, probably neighbors. She can't remember their faces, only the silence they left behind.

When she thinks of her husband, she can close her eyes and focus to will him away; he was not always a bad man, but she is tired of remembering.

She looks up. She is sitting on a bench, her mind clear, the memories dispelled. Next to her, a woman sketches the dollhouse. Her hands are long and curved; the pencil is like an extension of her arm. The proportions of the sketch are distorted, the image crude on the page.

The woman looks at her and closes her eyes. "I'm a collector," she says, answering an unasked question, then returns her attention to her work.

Major Shoemaker

American, 1915–2007

Horseradish Harvest, 1955

Oil on canvas

Although he would soon turn his attention to Neoplasticism, the cold, geometrically precise, nonrepresentational style associated with Piet Mondrian, here Shoemaker sheds the impressionism of his early career while still clinging to representational modes. Though the subject of the painting is articulated as if through a veil, the formal anxiety of *Horseradish Harvest* evinces the painter's metamorphosis. The painting is a rare example of the artist as *pupa*, Shoemaker no longer one thing, but not yet another.

One wonders why he bothered. The painting lacks reverence for the subject, as if Shoemaker, while painting, was distracted by something in the distance he had not yet grasped, something for which he yearned. Perhaps it's why he later abandoned this style altogether, opting instead to interrogate the geometry of pure form explored so thoroughly and with greater vision by other artists. Had he been more passionate, had he been better able to channel that passion through his hands onto the canvas, if he had been less intellectual, more visionary, perhaps then we would care about Shoemaker.

One of the only photographs I've ever seen of a young Shoemaker shows the artist smiling in his studio, his brush held to a blank canvas in a clearly posed shot, as if he were in love with nothing more than the idea that he might be seen as an artist. What would he think if he knew that we wished he had left the canvas blank?

Shoemaker continued to produce art sporadically until his death at ninety-two, after a long career both as a painter and a teacher, though in later photographs, Shoemaker's face is deeply wrinkled, his eyes wet and red, his lips in a tight frown hardened by so many years of trying to do something his eyes, brain, and hands simply could not do.

The Horseradish Lover's Cookbook is available in the gift shop.

Viviana van Weenen
American, 1953–2002

Defoliated, 1985
Pencil on paper

In the early '80s, van Weenen made a plan for a project in which she would defoliate a small section of trees in the woods of western Washington. She would drill into the naked and humiliated trees, cut their limbs, and finally girdle them, ensuring their eventual death.

Rather than perform the cruelty of torturing and murdering trees, van Weenen instead played out this obscene fantasy in the pages of her notebook, detailing each step of the project with stunning sketches, at once sublime and pornographic. Van Weenen also imagined photographing the patch of beautiful death from the sky and sketched what she speculated this would look like—a barren square of spindly wooden tendrils amid the lush rainforest.

Kermit Murdock

American, 1941–2013

Dear Greta, 1977

Oil on canvas

Dear Greta is one of Murdock's most unsettling paintings—Greta is barely a teenager here, though oddly, the model for this painting, the poet Greta Derwin, was in her fifties when she sat for this portrait, so it is difficult to call the work immoral or pornographic since the young girl is only a reimagining of the poet at a much younger age. The naked girl is not real, but a fiction created by the artist, and since the referent was a fifty-year-old woman, you may feel free to be stimulated without fear, shame, or discomfort.

Lola Lovett
American, 1971–

Prancers in the Moonlight, 1994
Gelatin silver print

A photograph of piglets cavorting after dusk is either ironic or something you would not typically find in an art museum, but here it is. *Prancers in the Moonlight* is technically and formally sound—notice the harmony of the prancers, the sharp focus, the rich contours of gray and black, the balance of timing and serendipity. The subject matter is banal and clichéd, however there is something sublime in this scene of animal joy, something at once childlike, serene, and wise. The scale of the photograph, enormous, larger than life, positions the viewer as small and bestial. We are stringy, base, and minuscule in the shadow of these young pigs. Are these creatures so far from us in their jubilation? Have we forgotten what it is like to feel the exuberance of a cool full moon on a summer night? We are no longer young and porcine.

Felicia Helsley
American, 1928–2014

Untitled, 1985
Acrylic and enamel on board

Imagine you can see through this painting to the wall behind it. Imagine the painting is a window. Imagine there is no painting at all, only a gold frame.

When you examine *Untitled* closely, when you lean in and the guards begin to approach you, you confirm it: there is nothing there but a wall smudged with dirt. Imagine now this card tells you *Untitled* is a statement about material and light.

I can tell you're not buying it.

How about this: this is art because it is framed, and hangs in a museum. This painting—this lack, this absence—is art because I chose to purchase it and hang it here. I have an advanced degree in art history on display in my office. We may have even paid a lot of money for it. Helsley's work hangs in other museums. You nod, though secretly you are thinking maybe this is a bit of a gimmick, maybe a practical joke played on not just you, the viewer, but also the museum, the curator, and perhaps even the artist.

Fritzina Redbrush
American, 1903–1981

King Crab VI, 1970
Oil on canvas

Fritzina Redbrush is believed to be a pseudonym shared by at least seven different painters who, through a collective living and working environment, attempted to create what they called a "seven-headed dragon," a persona that is all of the group at once, one of the group, and occasionally some or even none of the group. The group's anonymous manifesto, published as "The Fritzina Redbrush Papers," outlined their aesthetic and political goals and is mostly malarkey.

Multiple authorities have convincingly questioned the authenticity of *King Crab VI*. No documentation verifies that the Fritzina Redbrush collective really existed. Nobody has ever come forward to claim the two-dozen masterpieces the group allegedly made or their manifesto. Some authorities have accused the artists Fox and Shanks of creating the hoax. Many of the Redbrush paintings bear characteristics of both artists' work. If not perpetrators of a hoax, they were likely members of the collective.

When asked about Redbrush, Fox and Shanks claim that she was one person and that they'd met her on numerous occasions. At Redbrush's funeral, a line of artists, scholars, and critics extended around the block, and nearly all of them wept at the foot of her coffin. Fox claims Redbrush was killed when an industrial paper shredder got hold of her scarf, though a junior embalmer who worked on the Redbrush body claimed that the *real* Redbush murdered Fox and assumed her identity. Supporting this theory is the fact that Fox's notebooks are filled with sketches of king crabs and other crabs after 1981, the year of Redbrush's supposed death.

Believe what you want; I don't care—I love this painting. How menacing the claws of the mighty king crab!

Kaye Bannister

American, 1945–2005

The Descending Darkness, 2003

Oil on panel

Should you look? *The Descending Darkness* is a metaphor for the Cold War, for September 11th, for the war in Iraq, the war in Afghanistan; it is a metaphor for all war. For terror. For those who have died, and those of us who will die. The darkness that descends here is deep—and dark. You can see by the black, brown, gray and the murky crimson like dried blood. *The Descending Darkness* is a metaphor for consumerism, for capitalism, for kids today and for all the broken cats you have seen in the middle of the road with cracked bones struggling to crawl to safety. You swerved, you slowed down, you paused on the night road and wondered if you were capable of helping this thing.

The Descending Darkness is a metaphor for your first and third marriages, the desk you sit at, the monitor you look into when you are awake. It is sleepless nights, your spouse who snores so loudly you hope he chokes. The peaks of light-tinged paint, the bright edges, the deep slope down into the dark valley. The long strokes, this thick abyss.

It is certainly dark.

From afar, the painting looks like an exercise in smudges, the colors blending together to create a thick fog, though she is not reminded of violence.

She examines each brush stroke, paint thick on the panel, and admires the distinct edges of each deliberate movement of the artist's hand, the subtle transitions of color indistinguishable from afar.

Why has she come here? After so many years, walking by the museum on her way to the post office, on her way to city hall, on her way to sit in the gardens of the little college in summer, when the students have gone and she can be there alone. So many years ago, she would extend her time there, avoiding going home. She would walk among the empty buildings, look into the dark classrooms. Some days she could hear the band practicing in a distant field; some days, groups of students would emerge in swarms, scattering across campus, free from a punishing summer class.

Other days the campus was a ghost town, quiet and free. She loved those days. It was what the end of the world would feel like, she decided—quiet and still like Sunday morning.

For those who have died, and those of us who will die.

She thinks of a man she often sees in line at the post office, a man she doesn't know, but who shares part of her schedule. She thinks of his hands, mottled and gray with age like hers, but stronger, how he seems as if he might live forever.

She doesn't want to live forever, not anymore; she has already lived through so many deaths.

She has always thought the museum held something for her, something she didn't want, like a gift left by a loved one passed.

Artist Unknown

The Castle, ~1890s
Dollhouse from the Kendall Seagrave Memorial Dollhouse Collection
Gift of the Ambrose J. and Vivian T. Seagrave Family Trust

The Castle is the oldest dollhouse in the collection, likely dating from the 1890s. Though constructed of wood, this medieval fortress has been meticulously painted to appear as if it were stone. *The Castle* was purchased by Epaphroditus Cox, Vivian's father, in anticipation of her marriage to Ambrose, and was presented to Kendall after her baptism. Forbidden to touch her gift until her seventh birthday, Kendall was said to have been fascinated by the structure as a toddler—*The Castle* stood closed on a pedestal in the old lactation parlor adjacent to Kendall's dayroom, where she would sit enthralled by the windowless fortification. When she was old enough to play with the dollhouse, she focused her attention on the towers, where she imprisoned her dolls, and the dungeon, where she flayed her servants. Entrusted to our museum with the stipulation that the dollhouse be displayed as if Kendall could still play with it, we have set *The Castle* at a height so that viewers can see the subterranean dungeons (along with the tortured dolls and their smiling captors), which go three levels below the grounds. Though *The Castle* has been locked behind glass for decades, the dolls imprisoned in the towers occasionally switch positions with one another.

Iris Babbitt

American, 1940–2007

Horn of Plenty, 2001

Oil on canvas board

For months, *Horn of Plenty* hung on my living room wall, where I would gaze at it while listening to Babbitt murmur to me through the static of an unused AM radio station. Note the fingerprints visible in the thick paint, an unusual technique for Babbitt, whose fastidiousness kept her from sticking her fingers in anything, much less the deep slick of slowly drying oil. On this rare occasion, however, Babbitt used her index and middle fingers to gently massage the thick paste into peaks. I have since returned the painting to the museum, and at night, when I am especially lonely, I let myself into the gallery and in the darkness trace the path of Babbitt's fingertips with my own.

Toby Torez
American, 1925–1990

The Rusted Bridge, 1985
Acrylic on paper

Torez painted *The Rusted Bridge* before returning home to Pittsburgh to die. After decades in Paris, which he dubbed "the Pittsburgh of France," he longed for the soot-thick skies and corrosion of the real Pittsburgh, his last wish to see the skyline of his youth. Though he found Paris to be a mirror of his hometown in many ways—cuisine, culture, and attitude—he found little inspiration there beyond what he recognized of his home city. In *The Rusted Bridge*, Torez uses fractured geometric forms to suggest the dilapidation of memory; even in abstraction, one can see the splinters of nostalgia—there is a longing in these strange shapes, in the Rust Belt palette, and an uncanny sense of collapsing industry.

Hans Osterhagen

American, 1917–1999

The Swarm, 1947

Plaster

Gift of the Ambrose J. and Vivian T. Seagrave Family Trust

Osterhagen, a friend of the Seagrave family, was briefly implicated in Kendall Seagrave's disappearance before being cleared of all suspicion. Because of the family's guilt at the false accusations, Osterhagen was welcome to loiter endlessly in the estate gardens with all the other artists. Some afternoons there were so many sculptors and painters working in the garden, they themselves seemed like statuary. Vivian, in her black robes, and Ambrose, always in tails and top hat, lorded over them from the high balcony, pointing down as they worked as if to silently command their movement.

The Swarm depicts the inhabitants of the most splendid hive on the property in full swarm, each bee meticulously modeled and positioned to fly into the afternoon air. After his daughter's disappearance, Ambrose became an avid beekeeper, transforming much of the gardens into his personal apian empire. So common were bee stings among the artists who gathered there after Kendall Seagrave's disappearance and before Ambrose's untimely passing, Osterhagen and others came to wear full bee suits to avoid being stabbed by Seagrave's "angry children."

The artists in the garden as still statues, no longer free, but no longer burdened by the weight of art. A glimpse of cold stone moving only when she looks away.

No faces—only stiff gray bodies.

She feels a man standing behind her before she can see him. The silent specter makes no sound, seems not to breathe. She steps to the side and waits for him to move forward. Instead, he turns away and walks to the other side of the gallery.

She has lost sight of her childhood, only glimpsing it in dreams she is happy to quickly forget. What good comes of remembering, she thinks, when there is so much present. The boredom of old age—the routine, the loneliness—has slowed down what used to pass so quickly, entire years gone. The longer she lives, the longer her life seems to extend in front of her, the few years she might still have like all of her life again, compressed.

She looks away from the painting toward the man. He wears a blue suit, a hat, carries a flimsy canvas tote bag beside him. He holds his phone up to a painting, takes a picture, and moves on to the next.

A memory: standing in the kitchen, wet from the rain, begging her mother to allow her to stay. Her mother waited tables at a diner in town. It's still the same diner, still owned by the same family. She remembers how her mother moved them two counties away for better schools, how they lived in an apartment above a pool hall, above a dentist, above a family grocery, finally above another family in an old brick duplex. She remembers how happy the bright hallways of that last domicile made her every morning, how she would run the long corridors and hide in the shadows of the seemingly vast house. She recalls looking out the window, watching the downstairs neighbors' children playing in the backyard below on an old rusty swing set, how she could not wait to meet them. She remembers the feeling of the sand in the sandbox, building castles, playing hide-and-seek through the neighborhood at dusk, sitting alone with the older boy, his name long forgotten, beneath the canopy of an enormous pine.

She remembers the dark day they came and cut the pine tree down, the moving boxes all around her, ready, again, for a new beginning.

She remembers an alcove at the end of the hallway, a hollow in the wall, where she used to stand stone-still, posing like an idol in an apse.

She remembers her mother telling her when she was older how she didn't have a father, how she simply appeared to her one day; the joke makes her laugh still, though she knows now.

Enough of memories. She stands close to the sculpture, examines the exquisite detail of one of the bees, and wonders if an artist must love what he or she depicts, if it is enough simply to observe and translate from the eye to the hand.

The man pauses at the next painting, tilts his head as if he sees something in it, takes a step closer, leans to read the small print of the card, then looks up again at the painting, snaps a photograph, and walks away.

What is it like to lose a daughter and fall in love with bees, to surround oneself with people, to recover from a loss from which no one can recover—would not absolute loss have shattered him? How was he able to move on?

Men have killed themselves for less.

Gaylord Kellogg

American, 1891–1937

Nude in Crumbling Fortress #17, 1922

Oil on canvas

The seventeenth in Kellogg's *Nude in Crumbling Fortress* series yet again depicts a nude girl crouched in the rubble of a ruined citadel. Note the intricacies of the broken stone and how the window edges frame the scene, as if the viewer is looking over the old courtyard from a tower above, spying on the girl below. Note how the girl appears to be made of mist. Bathed in fragmented light, she is barely recognizable; she is a ghost, a smudge. She is paint.

Bryce Hammond

American, 1933–2009

Incremental, 1958

35 mm black-and-white film, sound, 6 min. loop

Hammond's first film work gestures toward classic Hollywood cinema distorted through an avant-garde lens. Begining [and ending] with the opening and closing of a camera shutter, the film is ostensibly the tragic story of a forbidden and doomed love affair, but it is also an exercise in making the abstract concrete, an experiment in visual representations of emptiness, and an exploration of the measurement of time through the metaphors of the tick, the click, and the blink.

Horatio Bautista
American, 1955–

Sierra de Grazalema, 1975
Oil on canvas

Born in Spain, Bautista moved to Los Angeles in 1970 with his mother, a much sought after trepanist. Throughout his early career, Bautista produced many landscapes of what he called his "beloved Andalucia," though most would agree the paintings look nothing like the region. Here, Bautista used the Wasatch Mountains as his model to produce this stunning range of snow-capped peaks.

Trevor David Sims

American 1943–1993 (presumed dead)

The Faithful, 1989

Acrylic on paper

While Sims is best known for the public attention brought about by his escape and subsequent deprogramming from a garbage-eating cult known as The Brethren, little attention has been paid to his painting. The secretive cult, known to live an ascetic and vagrant-like lifestyle, subsisted largely on cast-off scraps found in dumpsters. *The Faithful* depicts Sims's Brethren "family" as they forage for dinner behind a Cleveland, OH, Big Boy. It is one of only a few paintings documenting his time with The Brethren, though he produced many depictions of his new "family," the Detroit-based Extrasylvian Motor Aphasians, before the artist disappeared in 1993.

Squire John Ensign

American, 1865–1970

Common Labor, 1905

Oil on canvas

One of several Ensign railroad paintings in our collection, *Common Labor* depicts the aftermath of an all-too-common early twentieth-century accident: a worker has been crushed by a locomotive boiler that has fallen from its chains at an engine shop. Boiler-crushing was a common way to die before the invention of durable steel chain in 1935, and it was the railroad's custom to award deceased workers' families with lifetime, transferable passes that are still honored today by Amtrak and most freight lines, which will allow pass holders to sleep like hoboes in empty box cars, should they desire.

Over Ensign's extraordinarily long life and career, he almost exclusively painted railroading scenes, only occasionally exploring other modes of transportation and industry, and was to become known as the world's foremost chronicler of our nation's rich railroading heritage.

She sits on a bench to take in the scene: limbs and metal mangled, the horror of those-who-have-not-yet-died watching in awe of the weight of what they'd built. How privileged we are to no longer fear such death, to be liberated from such danger.

She thinks of faraway horrors, the violence of machinery, the wretchedness of work, the wickedness of our way of life in how we transfer and transport this violence to places we barely know, people we fail to imagine. How one life is always worth more than another life.

How our love for someone can be at the expense of another's love for someone else.

She is suddenly aware of music being played throughout the museum from overhead speakers. She doesn't at first feel offended by the soft violins, feels only the kind of violation that comes with subtle manipulation. She is suddenly ashamed of being here, in this bizarre and awkward space—the garishness of the enormous gift shop, the strangeness of so much art by people she has never heard of, the *soundtrack*.

She remembered when the construction of the museum was announced, how it promised to revitalize their ailing town by filling it with art and culture. Now, after finally visiting the place, she understood why it had failed to fulfill that promise.

Again she feels a presence behind her. A couple, hands together, distracted by something between them, something that has nothing to do with this place.

She remembers a train ride through one city on the way to another city, sitting in the window, her mother next to her, lost in a book. She remembers clutching her bear against her chest, looking out at a vacant lot littered with the rusty carcasses of some abandoned industry. A man in a white t-shirt held what looked like a gun to his head, waving to the train. He was gone before she knew if what she'd seen was real, before she could see what he was going to do.

She recalls that years later, on the same train route as an adult, she tried to spread cream cheese onto a bagel with an inadequate knife, plastic and flimsy. Looking out the window, she saw the vacant lot, now overgrown, still crowded with junk. Three children chased one another across the lot, shouting at the train.

She looks again at the painting. Her husband had worked in an office, taking the commuter train into the city, where he worried about what and how, about efficiency and margins, making decisions he called life and death even though they were neither.

They rarely left their little village, indistinct, like every place and no place at all. Linked by train to the city, but less an extension, and more like a residue. She was happy to leave it and all it held. They drove to get away to where they could be other people—drove to quaint inns, to resorts, to country restaurants exclusive and secluded. They took vacations to become other people, if only for a weekend. She'd liked the feeling, even if fleeting.

He'd had too much to drink, so she drove them, the roads empty because of the snow. A memory of headlights coming the wrong way slowly up the highway, of pumping the brakes, of sliding toward the other vehicle in slow motion. Their bumpers tapping, their seatbelts locking. The man was clearly drunk, but the police let him go, their cars barely damaged.

She looks again at the painting. We have fixed death, she thinks.

Roscoe Crooks (born Matthew Peuse)
American, 1930–2005

The Sarsaparilla Drinkers, 2004
Oil on canvas

A rugged scene of attractively robust and unwashed cattleman sharing sarsaparilla in the shelter of a grove of grand cottonwood trees, *The Sarsaparilla Drinkers* is a common Western scene in its representation of the fraternity of thirst-quenching after a hard day's work. The strangeness of the piece is found in the presence of tiny scorpions surrounding the men, their claws poised for attack, their tails perfect arcs, the tips of the arachnids' stingers careful swabs of umber so subtle as to render them nearly invisible against the dusty soil. The viewer may wonder how many stings the men can survive. I know that number to be at least sixteen; the men in the painting appear robust, but who knows what weaknesses are hidden from our eyes.

Attributed to **C. Seward**

American 1915–? [missing since 1975; presumed dead]

Untitled, date unknown

Bronze

This massive sculpture was recovered after a warehouse in which several of the enigmatic artist's sculptures were stored caught fire. Though this evidence suggests *Untitled* is by Seward, the artist himself could not remember making it. Shortly after the fire, Seward set sail from New York Harbor bound for Barbados in his father's antique sloop and was never seen again.

Untitled is atypical for Seward—who only sometimes worked in bronze and almost always cast human figures—in that it depicts a monstrous Cerberus. Post-inferno, the sculpture was displayed in the grand lobby of the Hotel Chesterfield in midtown Manhattan, but after guests regularly reported that the statue had eaten them in their dreams, the sculpture was sold to the museum, where it has been on display since.

Percy Shanks

American, 1933–

Ventriloquism, 2000

Acrylic on paper

Shanks, a notorious asshole, still inspires awe through subtle shifts in tone and luminescence and the collision of form and color smeared across substrates so expansive we can't see anything else. Viewers may ask why we devote so much gallery real estate to this man-sized turd, this womanizer, this art-world climber, but I cannot answer them because I am too busy at my desk, ignoring a phone call or an email to gaze through the skylight at a dead tree limb or a squirrel about to gut a walnut. I often think about closing the door of my office to extract my seed, but rarely do, and when somebody knocks, I'm glad to have thought better of it. On one wall of my office hangs a photograph of Shanks with his former lover, Miriam Fox, sitting like cool statues on a Manhattan rooftop. I'm told the person with Shanks in the photographs is an imposter—not Fox, but an impersonator so skilled Shanks himself didn't know the difference. Sometimes I wonder if the Fox we know is the real Fox, if she was replaced long ago, and if that is the case, what happened to her?

Caspar Richardson
American, 1901–1999

The Cosmic Dead, 1945
Oil on canvas

What the thief has stolen is not visible to the viewer of the painting, as is the constable who searches for him in the alley, shining his flashlight behind the crates and cans up and up onto the fire escapes above. What the thief has stolen he cups in his hands, and though a dab of black paint obscures half of his face, one can still see glints of awe in his eyes as he steps into the dense crowd of dirty workers walking home from the shovel factory steaming in the distance.

Richardson captures the peculiar energy that is the excitement of going home after ten hours in near darkness assembling tools in blistering heat. The workers are exhausted, but the lightness in their steps suggests there is nothing they would rather do than walk home on sewer-filled streets for a meal of tough meat and stale bread with their wives, weary too, and their children, who are just about old enough to begin their work.

Artist Unknown

The Summer Cottage, ~1920s

Dollhouse from the Kendall Seagrave Memorial Dollhouse Collection
Gift of the Ambrose J. and Vivian T. Seagrave Family Trust

Reputed to have been Kendall Seagrave's favorite dollhouse, *The Summer Cottage* shows signs of love in the broken and worn details—missing windowpanes and trim, chipped paint, a chimney clogged with a doll-sized turkey—but is still an exemplary specimen in its craftsmanship. Jokingly referred to as "The Summer Cottage," this colonial mansion is even bigger on the inside than it is on the outside, and it boasts a half-dozen bedrooms, three parlors, a library, and an enormous soaking bath complete with a copper basin big enough for five dolls. It's said that Kendall Seagrave would escape into this house for hours with her dolls and her imagination, concocting fantastic tales about a wealthy family that filled their home with love, adopting dozens of orphan children and dogs, abandoning their beaver-fur business in order to focus on animal welfare, improving the lives of the itinerant, and being kind to their friends and neighbors. Though it's unclear why Seagrave lost interest in this dollhouse, it was surely a source of affection for many years. Ambrose Seagrave stipulated in his will that this dollhouse be sealed shut after his death, and since then, it has never been opened. One can see the shadows of mysterious dolls lurking inside.

She is drawn to the dollhouses: ideal homes that never existed, cold and distant simulacra now broken and strange.

Through the windows, she searches the shadows, and enters like a ghost.

She remembers wandering the mansion as a child, running down the halls, how she hid in the still rooms while the sounds of her father's enormous voice echoed in the corridors, bouncing off the marble floors, off the bare walls. Looking through the window into one of the guest rooms, she can recall hiding in the dust beneath a bed, waiting for a storm to end, waiting until the heavy footsteps in the hallway had passed. She remembers the monstrous shadows lurking by the open door, remembers fearing they would come into the room.

She had no father, only her mother and dozens of tiny homes. They were always on the move, on the run from something she didn't understand.

She remembers longing for another life, longing for friends, longing for a pet dog, enormous and soft. She can remember the smell of the polish the maids used on her wooden bed frame, remember how at night, after dinner, she would sneak downstairs and one of the young cooks would give her cookies or share a cake the servants had baked for some celebration the family knew nothing about upstairs. If she concentrates, she can make the cook real. She can even remember her name.

Her mother would draw the bedroom blinds closed, leave the dim bedside light on, and lock the door, warning her not to make a sound. Her mother would tell her there was no such thing as ghosts, no such thing as monsters, but she knew better. Why else would her mother lock the door? After her shift, her mother would tiptoe into her room, gently wake her, and share a cookie or slice of cake she'd brought home from the restaurant.

She is suddenly dizzy, her head empty and heavy at the same time. She sits near the dollhouse and continues to look while she eats a pretzel from an open bag in her purse. She takes a sip of water and notices a guard eyeing her. She caps her water bottle, stands, walks around the dollhouse again. Now she can see all of the interior rooms, see the dolls inside, hear them speaking to one another. Money troubles, leveraged too high, limited liquidity. Her father too close to one of the artists. Another bothers her mother—a creep, she says. The artists are bringing too many of their friends, she says, hangers-on.

She can imagine how the sunlight came through the windows each morning in every room, how the sunsets looked from the west side of the house, her favorite perch in a plush chair in front of a window, in just the right spot, a good place to get lost in a book when the house was quiet, when no one was there.

When she was young, she used to imagine what it would be like to be old, wonder what it would be like to be alone. She has her health, someone told her, and that is enough, but it is never quite enough. One day her legs will give out, her heart, her liver. Every ache gradually worse, every weakness diminishing her: these things will not improve.

Liquid could fill her lungs and drown her from within.

Now, when she stands too quickly, her blood takes its time, her heart working to pump it to her frail extremities. She faints sometimes and knows *this* is what will kill her—a fall in the kitchen, her head against the edge of the counter, a fall down the basement stairs. She doesn't fear falling, doesn't fear suffering. When the end comes, she will savor it, knowing that even in pain, it will be the last thing she feels.

Kenneth Raney Clark

American, 1855–1940

Mother, 1910

Oil on canvas

Mother depicts Clark's mother supine and nude in a hammock stretched between two birch trees stripped of their bark. One might wonder about Clark's relationship with his mother based on the way she is posed in the painting. However, the erotic charge of the subject matter and the vibrant daubs of yellow, gold, and orange flowers surrounding her take one's attention away from the title of the painting and our (perhaps) troubled thoughts about Clark's sexual attraction to his parent. The unearthly quality of light here is particularly noteworthy, as are the bumblebees swarming around their hive in the crook of the tree on the left. We imagine Clark at work at his easel set haphazardly into the uneven ground of the meadow, while his mother, naked and wet with sweat, struggles to hold this position—her leg bent at the knee, her arms stretched above her head, her breast exposed to the hot afternoon sun, the bees menacing her above.

Iris Babbitt

American, 1940–2007

Bullets #9, 1971

Acrylic paint, sand, marbles, beaver and muskrat pelts, plywood

#9 is not Babbitt's best work, though its resistance to description is conceptually interesting. Despite its lack of appeal, it's something we can certainly have a conversation about. As a signed Babbitt, the piece is exceptionally rare because the artist foolishly refused to sign much of her work after 1965.

A decade ago, anticipating Babbitt's death and the subsequent interest in her work, I purchased several of her smallest assemblages—what I could then afford—and began to compile a catalogue raisonné of her works, a task that proved more difficult than I'd anticipated because the artist's own records were not well kept, though I was fortunate enough to acquire what she could provide: a box full of hand-written receipts going back decades. Because of the number of forgeries on the market and despite her failing memory, our conversations were critical for the authentication of hundreds of pieces. She passed away before I could complete the project, but a short time after she began to speak to me in dreams, telling me about what it was like to be dead, that her memory was sharp in the afterlife, and more usefully, she authenticated the remaining assemblages, though because of the surprising source of the information, only a few museums and collectors recognize the legitimacy of my transcriptions of her reports.

Erotic dreams I remember vividly were the precursor to her visits, visits that began one night while I relaxed in bed, about to begin my nightly meditation ritual. After a time, she began to visit me some mornings as I was waking, and also in my study, where she appeared, translucent but visible, sitting in an adjacent chair, relaxing and reading with me. We had long conversations, sometimes about art, sometimes about the world beyond the veil. I promised to keep the secrets of the dead, so cannot recount them here, but as the world's foremost authority on Babbitt, I am happy to report that since her passing we have become intimate friends and, if not inappropriate to admit here, lovers.

Though *Bullets #9* is not the best of the series, or even in the top third of her oeuvre, a fact she readily admits, it does nonetheless represent the beginning of an important transition in the artist's aesthetic, one that is likely boring to the casual observer, one that you probably wouldn't understand even if I explained it to you.

Wiley Cox
American, 1885–1960

The Owlbear, 1925
Bronze
Gift of the Ambrose J. and Vivian T. Seagrave Family Trust

One of a few works in the museum created by a member of the Seagrave family, "The Owlbear" is a monument to Cox's obsession with a mythical owl/bear hybrid he believed to inhabit the thick mountain forests of the northeast United States. The sculpture is among the only extant pieces of a man known more for his sexual attraction to and collection of statuary and dolls. Note the remarkable detail of the rippling muscles of the creature, the bulge of human-like genitals hinted at by the plume of feathery fur between the creature's legs, and the owlbear's long, sharp beak.

Viviana van Weenen
American, 1953–2002

List of Kings, 1975
Pencil on paper

Viviana van Weenen made this list, a list of all the kings she could think of, on a train trip between her home in Seattle and Chicago. Once in Chicago, she framed the list, which includes an impressive twenty-seven kings, and sold it to a gallery to fund the next leg of her journey. First purchasing a wooden crate, she drilled holes in the sides and, with the help of her younger brother, packed herself into it with enough supplies to last several weeks. Her brother shipped the crate to London, where she refilled her water containers and emptied her refuse; the crate was then forwarded to Moscow, then Tokyo, then San Francisco, and finally back to Seattle. In the darkness, van Weenen blindly sculpted hundreds of clay figurines of herself folded into the cramped container. Those sculptures, collectively known as *Folded Self*, are on display at another museum.

Imani Granger
American, 1920–2010

Apples and Gourd, 1941
Acrylic on plywood

Though best known for her stunning, expansive renderings of civil rights protests in the 1960s, this painting, likely completed during her last year of art school, is all we have.

Agnes Blunt
American, 1940–

Sick Room, 1985
Oil on canvas

Sick Room is Agnes Blunt's second most celebrated painting, a surreal yet hyperrealist reimagining of Munch's *Death in the Sickroom* in which several of the patients are depicted with the photo-realistic heads of old hounds. In Blunt's version, jocularity replaces the austerity of the original—no illness can quell the happiness of these dogs, despite their age and impending death. Blunt's fascination with Expressionist masters continued with many photo-realistic reinterpretations, hinting at a creative anxiety in finding her own subjects. These paintings of paintings, made using the canines of her mind as models, create conversations with the originals that we, as viewers of the works, cannot hear.

Anders Wilkinson
American, 1847–1905

Summer Day, Willow Grove, 1903
Oil on canvas
Gift of the Ambrose J. and Vivian T. Seagrave Family Trust

After Kendall Seagrave's disappearance, the Seagrave family went on an erratic buying spree that led to several odd purchases: the boat from which Kendall fell, for example, including all of the life preservers (only Kendall was wearing one), a collection of antique prison furnishings (housed in the museum's archives), hundreds of porcelain doll heads, and a seemingly unending number of poor-quality oil paintings, this one included. In it, one can see a fuzzy glen in the shade of what might have been beautiful willow trees had somebody who knew what they were doing painted them.

Gaylord Kellogg
American, 1891–1937

Nude Girl in Fragmented Light #6, 1925
Oil on canvas

Though we understand many figures in paintings to be derived from models, the figure here is purely a manifestation of Kellogg's intense reverence for his subject—nude girls trapped in the shadows of broken castle walls. His artistic genius is evident in the crisp realism of this fictional scene. While maintaining the ethereal and impressionistic qualities of the other works in the series, he was able to produce with *#6* a portrait that feels somehow *more real* than reality. If you could touch the canvas, you would feel the girl's skin, the subtle warmth of her body, and wish to free her from the painting.

Danielle Jenson
Canadian, 1923–2004

Monument, 2003
Watercolor and graphite on paper

Jenson said that her later paintings were attempts at a vision of "perfection," even though a close examination of the seemingly precise lines in *Monument* reveals imperfection. Lines intended to be parallel converge due to a misaligned ruler. Tick marks, meant as guides, remain. Tremulous lines, the product of Jenson's aging hand, are proof of how the body—the real—intrudes upon the ideal. From a distance, *Monument* might be seen as an achievement of Jenson's vision, but more interestingly, the presence of flaws calls into question the possibilities of precision and order while simultaneously suggesting perfection exists only in the artist's mind.

Tremulous lines. Like life, a precarious line.

She long ago gave up on the idea of anything resolving. Here she is.

Her hands tremble, have always trembled, but now the arthritis makes it difficult to grip a pencil, her fingers so often locking painfully. Only with concentration can she sign her name, but she need only write checks. She cannot remember the last time she has scrawled anything other than a promise of payment.

She had written in a daily diary, written letters and received them. She'd written to old friends, now far away, dead, or demented, written with her new address whenever she moved. Writing formed a line in a continuously shifting life.

She remembers the last time she moved, years ago, her husband dead—how she was drawn to this town again, how it felt somehow like a completion to return here, even though she'd never known a true home. Here, *she* would resolve.

She remembers turning forty, a line she'd crossed whereby her youth was now a *before*, everything that was to come an *after*, everything ahead complicated by what she would never be. After forty she foolishly waited to fall apart: back pain, sore neck, clogged veins. She had braced herself.

She'd looked at the bundles of letters held together with brittle rubber bands, the stacks of composition books in which she'd recorded her memories, volumes untouched for decades. One day, her husband away at a conference, she hauled the bundles to the backyard and piled them in the old fire pit, lit them, and watched the flames curl the brittle paper to ash. No more records hidden in the closet, no more remembering.

Her husband traveled as much as he could, always on a plane somewhere, always on a train, coming home late, sometimes stuck at the station until the wee hours. Sometimes he'd come home first thing, take the next day off, but more often he'd return to the office, sleep in his chair. That's what he said, but she wondered—something off in his voice on the pay phone, not enough background noise, too quick to say good-night.

They'd had nothing but one another. Late dinners in the light of the television, morning walks to the park, where they'd sit on a bench by the river with the newspaper between them, dinner in the city and a movie. Hadn't they had something, in their little routine?

She can see the motion of her own hands in the painter's marks, feel her steadying herself, futility fighting her own decay.

He had gone suddenly, in the night; though she'd found his body, it was as if he had vanished, his body not really *his*, but something for her to discover so she would not search.

So many people at his funeral, people she'd never met, people who would not speak to her. Even after he'd gone, he'd made her question what they'd had, what she'd meant to him.

When he'd changed the terms of their marriage, reduced it to a transaction, why had she stayed?

Why had she put up with so much rage, so many times, from so many men?

She'd turned to a new kind of writing in which she'd conjured a different life for herself, an opulent home, brothers, sisters, and children. She dreamed of a life without worry, without care, found solace in the imaginary. In notebooks, she built a new history, one of her own making.

She'd burnt those, too. Those fires were only ceremony—a celebration, the things inside now part of her new past.

Artist Unknown

The Victorian, ~1920s

Dollhouse from the Kendall Seagrave Memorial Dollhouse Collection
Gift of the Ambrose J. and Vivian T. Seagrave Family Trust

The Victorian is one of the finest examples of a post–World War I Victorian-style dollhouse in the western half of the state. Inside, one finds detailed furniture and meticulously crafted décor showcasing the period style and taste. Of particular interest here is the quality of the construction of the female dolls' clothes. The dolls can be found in the upper parlor, weaving lace together. Also of note is the tiny seascape—a miniature oil painting of tall ships—on the wall, flanked by the sewing women. In the dressing room off the master bedroom, an impressive collection of doll-sized shoes can be found arranged on a specially designed closet organizer. Kendall Seagrave was said to detest this dollhouse, though this is unconfirmed and unexplained.

Marian Bailey
American, 1932–

Aerial, 1965
Oil on canvas

Italian Futurism's influence on Bailey's *Aerial* is undeniable, though her contribution to aerial landscape is hard to classify. At the time she produced the painting, Bailey had never seen the ground from the air; her references were photographs and other aerial landscape paintings, especially those by Georgia O'Keefe, Susan Crile, and Hank Simmons, in addition to the works of Italian Futurists who commonly explored visions of the earth from the air. In *Aerial*, the sharp angles and distinct zones of color, reminiscent of the commercial art of the period, and the impression of falling motion, are combined in a style that is familiar, yet groundbreaking—the combination is so refined and uniquely Bailey's own that this work remains an unparalleled example of the genre.

Though typically aerial landscapes depict patchwork farmland or crumbling metropolises, Bailey rejects these tropes for a lofty view of her small hometown, as if she is plummeting toward her childhood. Whether from desire or force, we cannot tell.

Karl Tyler Fitch

American, 1895–1945

Mother and Daughter, 1943

Oil on canvas
Gift of the Ambrose J. and Vivian T. Seagrave Family Trust

Karl Tyler Fitch was one of two American soldiers executed for desertion during World War II, but he is best known as one of our region's finest prewar portraitists. For this rendering of Vivian and Kendall Seagrave, Vivian asked Fitch to portray her missing daughter as if she were in her late teens and about to be wed, so he depicted mother and daughter in fine gowns made by Italian designer Fausto Trotti. Using a mannequin in place of Kendall Seagrave, Fitch dutifully painted the mother and daughter to the best of his ability, but still, one can see the absence of animation in the ethereal, almost porcelain face of Kendall Seagrave. Though in life Kendall was often described as "doll-like," with "bisque" skin, here her pallor is corpse-like. Her mother's face, similarly drained of color, betrays the absence in the way she looks past her daughter, focused on Uncle Wiley, who watched while Fitch worked. One wonders what Mrs. Seagrave felt while sitting for the portrait, her fingers entwined with the cold fingers of a daughter she could only imagine. The painting was kept at the family's summer estate and was saved from a fire by Wiley Cox, who, after Vivian's death, kept the canvas tacked to a wall in his hunting cabin, where he was found dead in his bed.

Leroy Billings
American, 1940–2001

Girl in Hallway, 1965
Oil on canvas

In 1967, the girl pictured in *Girl in Hallway* allegedly walked out of the painting, followed a family home from the New York gallery where the piece was on display, and possessed the family's daughter, who over the course of three years tormented the family before finally smothering them with one of her mother's macramé pillows. A few days after the tragedy, the girl mysteriously reappeared in the painting, where she has, as far as anyone knows, remained to this day. The daughter lives in a hospital in upstate New York and has no memory of the painting or of offing her family. Billings, better known for his dramatic landscapes, here displays a creamy luminosity through his technique of layering paint and opaque glazes.

Girl in Hallway macramé pillows are available in the gift shop.

She has dreamt of falling out of the picture, dreamt of falling from a boat into the water, of swimming against the storm-current of a wide lake, washing up on shore. She has leapt from the top of a building, floated downward, then fallen hard and fast, only to awaken not before the moment of impact but after—jarred and broken, hemorrhaging—the dream following her into the waking world, her body stiff and sore. She has erased herself so many times, retreated to begin again; she has vanished and been reborn. Were she to disappear one last time, she would find a new place, somewhere quiet, a last refuge before death.

She dreams of the desert, a place without past or future, the amaranthine colors of the monolithic landscape changing without reference to geologic time.

The girl in the painting is pinned to the wall; she's looking out, her gaze held by something far away. She sees the girl peeling herself from the surface, the light shining through her translucent skin as she floats across the gallery, through the door, a representation released into the real. But here she is, planted firmly on the wall. Paintings are fixed visions, memories hardened on the canvas, the ghost of the child now trapped.

Annette Morgan
American, 1925–2011

Shopping Day, 1959
Oil on canvas

One of Morgan's first paintings in the exaggerated style for which she would later become renowned, *Shopping Day* presents a familiar scene, despite the broad expressions, distorted forms, and vigorous motion of the figures marching along a crowded street. Morgan's use of oversaturated color mimics the look of Technicolor film, and suggests an odd tension: *Shopping Day*, though painted during the period it depicts, feels nostalgic, as if Morgan predicted the coming cultural shift and chose to reinforce the stereotypes of 1950s American life before they were gone. The scene is so evocative of other overly nostalgic depictions of the era that some critics have suggested the painting is parodic, though the artist claimed it to be a sincere rendering of people she loved. Other critics have argued that the power of this and other similar works by Morgan is that they represent how people recall their own lives in the period, as if the painted images have become, for some viewers, memories.

Trevor David Sims
American, 1943–1993 [presumed dead]

Infinite Regret Hole, 1992
Oil on canvas

The only known Sims work done with oil paint on canvas, materials the artist said were "too rich," preferring instead to work on salvaged paper with student-quality acrylic paints. This is also the last known painting by Sims before his 1993 disappearance, attributed to his disillusionment after joining the Extrasylvian Motor Aphasians, which turned out to be just another cult. Though a witness claimed to have seen the artist at a highway rest area near Cheyenne, Wyoming, *Infinite Regret Hole*, even in its abstraction, tells another story—suggesting the motion of falling, as if the viewer is about to step over the edge of the painting and succumb to the void of infinite sorrow and darkness.

Kenneth Raney Clark
American, 1855–1940

Carapace, 1939
Oil on wood

On the threshold of knowledge, you stand before this empty shell and gaze upon the luster inside, the true beauty of this imaginary tortoise exposed only in death.

Iris Babbitt

American, 1940–2007

Seventeen Swans, 2007

Watercolor and charcoal on paper

The last known Babbitt, *Seventeen Swans* is little more than a stain left by the artist's spirit in the days before it left her body, flew through the paper, and evaporated into the ethereal beauty with which I would fall in love.

Though now her presence in my house is only a nuisance, like the smell of something once delicious that has rotted in the refrigerator, for a moment our love transcended physicality and the waking world. Our time together was most real when I dreamt. In sleep, we could go to dinner, hold hands, walk through the park together. I could watch her paint, praising her when she was a genius, and chastising her when she was anything but.

In one particular dream, she had occasion to accompany me to a conference for the curators of regional American art museums. I was nervous because I had been invited to give a talk, but also delighted to present Babbitt's ghost as my date to the banquet. On the flight back, Babbitt insisted on folding herself into the luggage bin above my seat, quietly moaning for the entire flight. The passenger sitting behind me told me he could see what looked like worms crawling across the surface of my skull. I wondered if the worms had been there for years, if they were only now visible through my thinning hair. I wondered what they were doing there, what they meant.

I don't remember the talk I gave at the conference, except that it had to do with the conflict between the perceived value of a work and its larger role in the narrative of the museum and the region. I wanted to talk about the curator's responsibility to not only annotate every work on display, but also to tell a story—not necessarily the story of a place, but certainly the story of a changing firmament, the arrangement of works like a constellation of stars.

Gilbert "Bucket" Wilson

American, 1938–1987

Untitled, ~1960s

Latex paint, cow's hair, blood, wallpaper on plywood

Gilbert Wilson, known to locals as "Bucket," was for years in charge of smashing cows' heads with a sledgehammer at the United Home Dressed Meats slaughterhouse on 31st Street. Old timers will recall how the stream next to the slaughterhouse would run red by evening, delighting the children who swam there.

After Wilson's death, over a hundred works on plywood were found in the shed behind the shack in which he lived. Many are nonrepresentational collages, like this one, though a few are extremely disturbing portraits of headless men engaged in unspeakable acts. In 1995, the museum mounted the first exhibition of Wilson's work, focusing on the most upsetting of his collages. So traumatic was the experience of viewing his work in volume, attendance waned, and the show closed after only three weeks.

Recently, Wilson was posthumously convicted and ceremonially executed for several unsolved murders.

Artist Unknown

City Hall, ~1930s
Dollhouse from the Kendall Seagrave Memorial Dollhouse Collection
Gift of the Ambrose J. and Vivian T. Seagrave Family Trust

City Hall was one of Kendall Seagrave's least favorite dollhouses due to the cold bureaucratic feel of the government building. She dutifully arranged suited clerks, administrators, and an ombudsman in the marble halls of the neoclassical structure, but only visited if one of her dolls needed to pay a parking ticket or apply for a building permit. In the months before her disappearance, *City Hall* mysteriously caught fire and was restored by the Seagrave family.

Harry Rankin
American, 1945–2001

The Sugarmakers, 1980
Oil on wood

The oversaturated colors and serpentine shapes of the figures walking through the snowy woods suggest a nightmare, though the scene itself is one of simple labor—collecting sap on a cold morning. Thick strokes of paint and the gouges made with Rankin's palette knife contribute to the painting's sense of horror, the marks reminding us that the woods depicted are still wild, that where sap is gathered lurks danger (e.g., wolves, snakes, ghosts). The exceptional size of *The Sugarmakers*, its simple materials, its inclusion of human figures, and its New England setting make this painting atypical of Rankin's work from this period.

Annette Morgan
American, 1925–2011

Children's Day #3, 1973
Oil on canvas

In this, the third painting of the series, Morgan again depicts children happily assembling electronic toys in a dimly lit factory. However, the expressions of joy on the faces of these seeming Christmas elves appear forced, as if they are smiling on command. The viewer becomes complicit in the painting's point of view: we observe from above as if we are the children's captors, their elation a balm for our guilt, our love of new things fulfilled at the expense of coerced labor.

Theophilus Harding

American, 1897–1945

Kendall Seagrave with Flute #1, 1942

Oil on canvas

Gift of the Ambrose J. and Vivian T. Seagrave Family Trust

Harding's portrait of Kendall Seagrave holding a flute echoes Vermeer's *Girl with a Flute*, though nobody would seriously compare the two paintings. Harding's understanding of light and composition was lacking [to be generous], and it is said that the resemblance to Kendall was so poor that the family refused to display the portrait until long after her disappearance, when anything associated with their missing daughter became an object of great value. In her diary, Vivian Seagrave noted that though the girl in the painting did not share a likeness with Kendall, she could see her daughter's light in the girl's eyes, and knowing that Kendall sat patiently for hours holding a flute—an instrument she never played—imbued the painting with an aura she could not deny. She could feel her daughter's presence through Harding's hand.

Along with the dollhouses on display in the museum, *Kendall Seagrave with Flute #1* anchored the Seagraves' collection, forming the core of the museum's collection at its founding. Continued financial support from the family, via a trust formed specifically for the purpose, allowed the museum to expand, gradually blossoming into the bouquet you see today.

The child with the wet hands emerges from behind a gallery wall, his face covered in jam. He flits around the room, hiding behind a blob of bronze, peaking, sneering. He extends his foot, and then his leg, skulking toward her, then pivots, pauses, and runs into the next gallery.

A man stands behind her, looking over her shoulder, examining the painting, examining her; she can feel his gaze on her shoulders, the right side of her face. She notices a metal ash can tucked into the corner of the room and wonders if it is something to consider—a conceptual piece, unmarked, the sand in the top smooth, white, crystalline—or if it is simply a relic.

Can it be both, she asks, on the verge of a thought when she notices a smudge of what looks like blood on the back of her hand. The ocher smear is dry, brittle, somehow the wrong color. She rubs at the flecks with her fingers, flicks them away, then checks her arms, pulls her long skirt up to inspect her calves and shins, and there on the top of her foot is another smudge, redder, still wet, a single drop of blood without a cut. She finds a tissue in her purse, wipes the drop, checks her arms again, looks at her face in her mirror; nothing.

The man has stepped around to her side. He scratches his chin, reads the card, takes a photo. He's wearing a pinstriped suit a size too small. His belly, stuffed into a crisp white dress shirt, hangs over the tight belt. His sleeves end an inch too high. He seems uncomfortable, out of place. He looks at her, looks at the girl in the painting, looks then at the ashtray; he has seen something, she thinks, but is not sure what.

She could see her daughter's light in the girl's eyes; she cannot fathom this, cannot fathom a daughter.

She opens the crumpled tissue, examines the smudge of color, again examines herself for a cut somewhere on her body or face. She touches the back of her neck, her hand stopping on the bump of a mole, maybe a bit bigger this time than when she felt it last. She finds the line where her skin meets her hair, thin and brittle.

She tries to imagine: she'd had a daughter with her husband; maybe that daughter had grown up hating her, grown up hating her father, grown away from them—moved away, engineering a kind of death, starting a new life somewhere else, parentless, an orphan, alone and free. Maybe her daughter has led the life she had wanted for herself, somewhere warm, somewhere fabulous, doing amazing things.

She can imagine the light of her daughter's eyes in a likeness not like her at all, a yearning so vivid it could replace the real memory.

For the first time in twenty-two years she considers buying a pack of cigarettes; what harm could they do her now?

Gaylord Kellogg

American, 1891–1937

The March, 1924

Oil on canvas

Some Kellogg scholars believe this is one of his last really *good* paintings, that his later, post-1927 paintings lack something, either simply from the artist aging or because so deeply was his life touched by the horrific events of 1927 that he lost some combination of his inspiration, talent, and work ethic. The details of the tragedy can be found easily via other sources, but why be coy? It seems unfair to suggest in a museum that visitors go elsewhere for information. In the spring of 1927, on a hiking trip in a remote area of southern Utah, Kellogg's two sons become stuck waist-deep in memory mud while playing near their campsite. As recounted later to authorities, Kellogg's wife, and then Kellogg himself, waded into the mud to retrieve them but became stuck themselves, lost in the gyre of their past. Several hours into the night, his youngest and admittedly weakest became glass-eyed, stuck in the loop of memory. His second son followed, and by morning, his wife, too, was vacant-eyed and unresponsive. Kellogg, mired only a few feet from his dead family, watched helplessly as bald eagles began to circle his comatose family, hollowed and lost.

Inexplicably, Kellogg himself was spared. Though not relevant, it is interesting that a donkey will get stuck in memory mud while a mule will not.

In *The March*, Kellogg showcases his pre-1927 style at its height in the five figures, eroded and insectlike, walking toward an unearthly sunset. The crudely hewn figures, slender and gnarled, suggest the people walking toward darkness have been stripped of nearly everything, humans whose souls have long left their diminished bodies. The painting is strangely prescient, as if Kellogg knew what would befall his family.

Gaylord Kellogg

Fergus Wood
American, 1950–1989

Helicopter Party, 1972
Oil on canvas

Wood's ability to ironically capture upper-class malaise through crooked scenes of haplessness is on fine display in this crowd of shirtless WASP lads shoehorned into a chopper. Wood perfectly records the boys' happiness, their bodies pressed together and wet from the drinks they've spilled while the horror of what is about to happen is betrayed by the pilot's face and the seemingly rapidly approaching grounds of the boys' estate seen through the side window of the helicopter.

Falco Medina
American, 1936–1983

Alkaloid Nightmare, 1966
Scrap

Medina's *Alkaloid Nightmare* would be of interest to any scholar of American monumental minimalism were it monumental or minimal. Despite the artist's best efforts, this jarring heap of metal is monstrously bad. Though Medina's allegedly blistering affair with artist Iris Babbitt brought him and his work some attention, my conversations with Babbitt reveal that he was an impotent meatball who affixed himself to her for personal gain. Over many years I have been slowly dismantling this pile of trash as if it were Medina's own body, methodically pruning each nut, screw, and shard, jubilantly tossing them into the river on my way home from work.

Artist Unknown

The Grand Hotel, ~1930s

Dollhouse from the Kendall Seagrave Memorial Dollhouse Collection
Gift of the Ambrose J. and Vivian T. Seagrave Family Trust

The Grand Hotel, the most elaborate and largest dollhouse in the collection, filled an entire room at the Seagrave estate and was so expensive Kendall was only permitted to play with it under the supervision of her wet nurse. Kendall loved to arrange the guest dolls and the staff dolls in the vast chambers, peering at them from above while imagining their lives—their jobs, their friends, their loves, and their affairs. Like those on the Seagrave estate, the rooms and outbuildings of *The Grand Hotel* are connected by secret doors and tunnels. The original purpose of them has long been forgotten; however, visitors to the hotel made use of them, under Kendall's direction, to conduct secret business. One speculates they served a similar purpose on the estate, something Kendall may have been aware of.

Clifford Vernon
American, 1863–1935

Torrent of Now, 1920
Oil on canvas

Vernon's painting is an example of Atavistic Futurism, an obscure movement centered around a dozen artists working in post–World War I western Pennsylvania and Ohio who sought to depict the future as it might have been predicted by those from the distant past. Like the Italian Futurists, the Atavistic Futurists were interested in speed and innovation, though unlike their Italian counterparts, they had witnessed the horrors of World War I and were committed to peace and utopian concepts. *Torrent of Now* is exemplary in that it achieves a vision of the future using a combination of so-called primitive techniques, like blowing pigment onto a substrate. The painting also embraces Cubism and Art Deco. The subject—a fleet of stone airplanes conceived by an artist pretending he had never seen modern machines—is unfortunate and bizarre, if vibrant.

Hatti Mendoza

American, 1965–

Wintery Mix, 2005

Oil on canvas

Wintery Mix is one of the most contemporary works on display, one of our last purchases before it became necessary to stop wanton spending lest the museum bankrupt the trust that keeps us open. Though created recently, the painting could be mistaken for a lost example of early twentieth-century Delaware Impressionism, down to the specifics of the pigmentss used. Mendoza achieved some early acclaim for her installations, but found commercial success with her series of imitations of Delaware school painters. Here, note how various elements seemingly obscured by a gauze of snow and rain nevertheless shine through the bleak curtain—the child's wagon upended in the street, the mountain lion disappearing into the forest with a chicken in its mouth, the farmer's wife sneaking into the parsonage; Mendoza's eye for detail and skill with the brush make her one of the greatest American painters of the 1940s.

Horace Paul McNamara

American, 1858–1945

***Portrait of Kendall Seagrave*, 1933**

Oil on canvas

Gift of the Ambrose J. and Vivian T. Seagrave Family Trust

One of our region's most eminent pre-1950 portraitists, McNamara was commissioned by Vivian Seagrave to paint her infant daughter, producing this stunning vision of childhood innocence and beauty. Dressed in white flowing lace and bathed in morning sun, Kendall lifts to the light a face that appears so heavenly the sky could open at any moment and take her back to the clouds. Vivian was rumored to have been unhappy with the portrait because, she claimed, it looked nothing like her daughter. McNamara struggled to revise the child's visage, but nothing he could do satisfied her mother until he used the face of a man from a French hosiery advertisement as his model.

What happens to the body when it suffocates?

The girl in the painting is lifeless. She is posed, put in place and moved by someone's hands, positioned like a mannequin in a store window.

Taking a drink of water, she remembers floating in a cold lake while catching her breath, shouts from far away, carried over the choppy water on heavy wind.

And then she swam, her sloppy stroke draining her, the shore still so distant.

She swallows water, panics, loses her rhythm, her strength; she tries to find the bottom of the lake with her feet, flushes at the sudden feeling of being alone in the frigid expanse, suspended in liquid, no air reaching her lungs. The water invades her, tries to take her, to become her, pulling her down. She coughs the water up, feels sand on her tongue, scratching her throat. A tangle of weeds entwines her like a conspiracy. Desperate to breathe, desperate for warmth and land, she coughs again, sucks air through her nose, takes as much as she can muster. She lies back, spreads her arms and legs wide, returns to her breath, pushes away the fear, the dread of drowning, wills energy to her limbs, at peace with a whole world of water.

The girl haunts her, this portrait-that-is-not. She is troubled by this invisible collage of model and likeness, the alien light, the false face, the edges of the imaginary undetectable.

The girl follows her as she walks away, follows her into the restroom, where she splashes cold water on her face, drying off with a stiff brown paper towel. She avoids the mirror, instead leaning against the sink, facing the empty stalls. The air conditioner hums, fills the chamber like a chorus.

Feeling a drop of water below her left nostril, she dabs it dry, looks down at the paper towel and sees a spot of blood, not red but burnt brown and orange, her body leaking unnatural liquid. She closes her eyes, turns and leans toward the mirror, opening her eyes but avoiding her own gaze, to find her face clean and dry, her nose no longer bleeding.

Viviana van Weenen
American, 1953–2002

The Coin Eater, 2010
Gelatin silver prints (5)

Viviana van Weenen swallows a dime, and then a nickel, before having her left ring finger amputated by a German surgeon in this series of photographs.

Van Weenen's sculpture *Finger*, on display elsewhere, features the artist's amputated digit in a mason jar full of formaldehyde, along with a dime, a nickel, and a tiny preserved turtle.

Kenneth Raney Clark
American, 1855–1940

Mountain and Sky, 1937
Oil on canvas

This painting, like every other landscape in which imposing slate mountains rise to meet a dusk-red sky, depicts nothing you have seen before, yet is also an image of something you have often seen—a romanticized rendering of pastoral bliss, an ominous mountain pass, an impressive American vista, the seemingly infinite reproduction of dramatic topography. Though the mountain and sky in *Mountain and Sky* may exist somewhere west of here, Clark never saw it, instead copying the scene from a photograph of a black-and-white painting he'd found in a book. Clark often looked to photographs of other paintings for inspiration, saving him the toil and exertion of trekking into the wild with his paints and easel.

Squire John Ensign
American, 1865–1970

Ghost Train, 1965
Oil on canvas

Late in his career, during what some critics generously refer to as his "blue period," Ensign began to experiment with color and form in ways that saw him moving away from the bright realism that plagued most of his career. Here, Ensign depicts a rusted steam locomotive emerging from a tunnel in a cloud of thick turquoise smoke.

Attributed to **Milton Waxcomb**
American, 1890–1945

The Townhouse, ~1932
Dollhouse from the Kendall Seagrave Memorial Dollhouse Collection
Gift of the Ambrose J. and Vivian T. Seagrave Family Trust

Modeled after a seventeenth century English townhouse in the Georgian style, this piece was claimed by the Seagrave family to have been commissioned from famed dollhouse maker Milton Waxcomb on the occasion of Kendall Seagrave's first birthday. No record of the dollhouse exists in Waxcomb's meticulous papers. *The Townhouse* was reputed to have been Kendall Seagrave's favorite of her dozens of dollhouses. A couple of her favorite dolls can be seen dining on breakfast scones and tea in the parlor. One can only imagine what they're talking about, though from the look on Father's face, it can't be good. Perhaps there has been a poor beaver harvest, or perhaps he is angry that his wife has produced only female children.

Iris Babbitt

American, 1940–2007

Untitled 12, 2006

Acrylic and sand on velvet

I can only imagine what you see when you look at this taint; I'm reminded only of Babbitt's final journey and the awful month that transpired before her spirit was at last set free from the world.

Babbitt's ghost had become very angry. We hadn't spoken in weeks. Days went by without me hearing or seeing her, and then, just as I fell asleep, I would hear her wretched moans as she commenced to detune the cello and play terrible songs, spoil the food in the refrigerator, or scatter the stuffing from the mattress and all the pillows. Her hauntings would diminish for a time, then begin again with intensity and increased frequency. She pulled nails from the floorboards, chewed holes through the walls, and cut the lamps' power cords. One morning I awoke to find she had broken the windows at night, scattered the glass across the bedroom floor, and hidden my slippers.

One morning, while I shaved and combed my hair, she cracked the mirror, and later that day, when I came home from work, I felt for the first time her cold hands grasping my ankles from beneath the bed.

In situations where one finds oneself in the company of unwanted spirits, it is customary to call upon a priest or other such authority on the supernatural, but I remained steadfast in my love for Babbitt and pledged to her angry ghost to never betray her, even as she brought a crystal vase down upon my head from its home atop Grandmother's highboy. I pledged again when I found the living room draperies suddenly aflame, and again when I found the Dachshunds (both named Iris) floating in the overfilled tub, and once more as she dragged me by the ankles up and down the staircase.

My body and mind had been abused to the point where it was no longer possible to love Babbitt, though in retrospect I realize that *I did—and do*—still love her, but that she had made it impossible for us to continue. The abuse her restless spirit inflicted on me was her way of communicating, perhaps in the only way she knew how. It was her letting go.

After a period of mourning, I was finally able to take *Untitled 12*, a terrible mess of a piece—without vision, style, or even a signature to help validate its provenance—from its place in the dining room to its current home in the museum for the public to enjoy or lambaste as they see fit.

Gaylord Kellogg

American, 1891–1937

Hanging Blouses, 1927

Oil on plywood with cotton, taffeta, nails, aluminum

Hanging Blouses was created at the end of Kellogg's self-imposed exile, the bulk of which he spent in a drafty barn near the town of Bivalve on the Eastern Shore of Maryland. Though he produced some art in his studio in the barn's loft, he spent most of his days crabbing and meditating on the tragic events of 1924. In *Blouses* we see Kellogg fully incorporating nontraditional materials—bits of cloth and hardware—into paintings that were decreasingly realistic, though here one can perceive women's blouses hanging on a clothesline in an otherwise empty field of what could only be wheat. One cannot help but wonder: to whom do these blouses belong? It is difficult to disassociate the blouses—empty clothes hanging far away, it seems, from any domestic space, inexplicably left in a wheat field—with the tragedy that befell the Kellogg family. The distant crows, witnesses to the terrible emptiness, are the only sign of life.

Why taffeta? Why crows? I don't know the answers to these questions, but regardless, this is one of Kellogg's worst paintings; imagine, gluing bits of cloth to an otherwise fine landscape.

Maud Taylor
American, 1887–1969

The Honeymooners, 1935
Oil on canvas

Maud Taylor, a minor figure in the Harlem Renaissance, was mostly ignored during her lifetime and remained relatively unnoticed until a recent surge in critical interest in her work. Though in need of cleaning and repair, *The Honeymooners* draws steady interest from visiting scholars, who stare at it hoping to gain some insight into the life and mind of this mostly undocumented artist. Because of these esteemed visitors, many of whom come on junkets funded by the most prestigious universities in the world, our small town enjoys a singularly high-quality restaurant, one that could not exist otherwise. Do not be intimidated by the old, bespectacled man gazing into the canvas as if he were looking through it, taking notes in a leather-bound notebook for another thin Taylor monograph. Instead, enjoy the spirit of the subject—a couple on a train, presumably on their way to their honeymoon. Instead, enjoy the exquisite light and texture of this especially fine painting.

Though our gift shop sells postcards of *The Honeymooners*, we are often out of stock.

Curtis Hornthwaller

American, 1955–

The Swallowing, 1980

Oil on canvas

Hornthwaller's least erotic painting, *The Swallowing*, is still very erotic. Viewers sometimes find the graphic subject matter upsetting, but most are secretly aroused, if not enthralled, by the vibrant explosion of color and energy. Many of Hornthwaller's works depict orgies, and though this isn't considered one of his major paintings, the sheer amount of blood displayed here—on the bodies of the figures, but also staining the mattresses and walls—is unusual. Of particular interest is the naked woman, reminiscent of a young Iris Babbitt, her fingers extended forward as if in a trance, standing at the edge of the composition, near the frame, as if she has only just arrived. Though ecstatic, she is unsure of what to do; if only I were there to show her. If only I could walk through the window of the painting and into her arms. I stare at *The Swallowing* at night, peering into her eyes, trying to will her into existence, or myself out of it.

How lonely the man who writes these cards must be to love a ghost. Maybe the trace of a person is easier to love than the real thing, the imagination overcoming reality, the mind compensating for unbearable isolation by summoning a phantom.

She has loved images before: faces on screen, in photographs, memories of the ones that got away: a dear friend in college who loved her, who met someone else before she realized what might have been. A coworker at her first job out of school, an accountant she met on the train, a rare books librarian, a glance from across the grocery store, the glimpse of a face in a car next to her stopped at a red light. What could have been: other lives, different memories, a fracture in time, spiraling away. Where she could have ended up, where she might be now, instead of standing here, looking at this painting, a fantasy of the curator.

Why so much blood? On the mattress, on the walls. Yet the woman standing at the edge of the room, naked for some reason, has skin so pearlescent she could never exist in real life. This woman, these painted women, treasures of the museum, figments of sad men.

Two men stroll up behind her. She can feel their eyes on her back. One of them whispers while the other giggles. Were she younger, she would have felt shame hearing men laugh at something—questioned her shape, her dress, her hair, her shoes—but she can ignore them now. They are nothing to her, just two men in a museum. How nice it must be to never grow old.

The curator must look so strange here at night, sitting on a folding chair, staring at the painting with the lights all but off. She imagines him trying to will the woman into existence through the force of his desire.

When she is alone in her bed in the dark she remembers the ones-that-got-away and tries to create them, too. She can trace the trajectories of their lives together, each night a different one.

The art in the museum is not so bad, she thinks, though it is strange to know so few of the artists, yet to feel like she has seen so many of the works before.

The men have stopped in front of a painting; one of them points, and the other puts his hand on his companion's shoulder, bends forward, laughs too much. What they are looking at could not possibly be as funny as his body would suggest. Maybe they were not giggling at anyone's expense; maybe they are simply in love, every experience together a detonation, every moment crackling and extraordinary.

Daniel Holloway

American, 1895–1943

The Hand Extends, 1935

Oil on canvas

The Hand Extends depicts three figures, two of which are engaged in the act of eating the third. The painting has an interesting history: its first owner, who commissioned the work from Holloway, was savaged by dogs after owning the painting for a year; the second bled to death through his pores only three years after hanging the piece in his Manhattan penthouse; the third owner threw himself into a volcano. Subsequent provenance for the painting is hazy, for though *The Hand Extends* was infamous, it disappeared for decades, finally coming up at auction in London in 1979. From that time until 1983, the work was displayed in a private gallery in Yorkshire, where the gallery owner sawed his feet off at his ankles, made broth from his own bones, froze the broth, and a year later used it as an ingredient in a vichyssoise, which he served at a dinner party. A tornado destroyed the gallery in 1983, killing the owner and reportedly destroying *The Hand Extends*, along with several important early works by Kellogg, Babbitt, and Hornthwaller. Upon learning the history of *The Hand Extends* in a mail-order course on cursed art, I was delighted when the painting materialized at auction in Singapore in 1991. I happily purchased the piece, and after cleaning and restoring the painting, displayed it in the museum for years without incident. When viewers reported various symptoms, including circadian dysrhythmia and false memories, I felt compelled to cover the painting with the black curtain that hides it today.

Please do not look behind the curtain.

Luella Dewey

American, 1865–1917

March for Geoffrey: The Golden Caravel, 1902

Oil on canvas

Gift of the Ambrose J. and Vivian T. Seagrave Family Trust

Dewey, loosely associated with Tonalism throughout her career, here stays true to that style in the ghostly, mystical scene of a ship on a foggy night. Despite the fact that one can barely discern the Golden Caravel emerging from a mist of paint, even in good light, this painting is often cited on the comment cards as patrons' favorite in the museum. Mrs. Seagrave loved this one, too, and demanded it be displayed prominently. It is certainly competent, and a crowd pleaser, but that does not make it transcendent.

Juniper Snyder

American, 1905–1985

The Neighbors, 1935

Acrylic on canvas

Gift of the Ambrose J. and Vivian T. Seagrave Family Trust

Snyder, a regional landscape painter of no note, befriended the Seagrave family and could often be seen in the gardens with her sketchbook, drawing various plants and birds she found there. Snyder became such a fixture at the Seagrave's estate that she was dubbed their "second daughter" by locals, though in truth she rarely interacted with the family. Certainly the Seagraves liked to surround themselves with artists and writers of questionable merit, and Snyder is another on that long list. Like no other, however, she unwittingly captured the dullness of life on the estate through her use of bland, lukewarm colors to render muted light, her uninteresting compositions, and a general lack of artistic judgment.

The Neighbors is a rare Snyder portrait, and rarer still because it appears to have been created off the estate grounds, since these "neighbors" would hardly have been invited anywhere near the gardens. Snyder likely painted this couple near her own home, across the railroad tracks on the west side of town. One can see the souls of these good, hard-working people—likely employees of the old shovel factory—through the deep lines on their faces, the dirt caked in those wrinkles like the cracks in a dry, fallow field.

Geraldine Andrews
American, 1865–1947

The Leather Menders, 1945
Oil on canvas

Though entirely abstract, *The Leather Menders* depicts two women mending leather pants surrounded by an empty basket, a basket filled with knitting, an open bag, another basket, a pair of mismatched shoes, a cut persimmon and papaya, a peeled banana, a baby in a bassinet, a bowl of oysters, a fish wrapped in newspaper, and a naked log. On the table between them is an enormous, gaping melon, and on the wall behind them a drawing of a sperm whale suggests that the women's husbands are away on a whaling ship. Their hats lay in their laps and though busy with their work, the women seem to enjoy one another's company, happy and seemingly unafraid for their whaling men, away risking their lives harvesting spermaceti.

Mitsuto Matsui
American, 1965–

Heap #3, 2001
Found objects

Matsui was trained as a painter but became interested in using found objects in his work, especially for producing commodity sculpture, shortly after graduating art school and moving to Chicago. Though he found quick and steady demand for his horse paintings, his passion was in creating sculptures from discarded office paper and shredded documents. He constructed his *Heap* series from these materials, using broken desk chairs as pedestals, fixing each piece to the next with a powerful adhesive of his own invention. *Heap #3* is regarded by many to be one of his finest heaps because of its enormity, but also because of its symmetry and craftsmanship. Matsui is often referred to as a critic of modern American office culture—many of his sculptures seem to cynically comment on the failure of the dream of a "paperless office"—but here, he seems to be celebrating capitalism, commerce, and waste, creating a monument rather than a critique.

Gaylord Kellogg
American, 1891–1937

Nude in Crumbling Fortress #25, 1923
Oil on canvas

In *#25*, the penultimate in the regrettably long series, one can still discern the edges of what might arguably be the stony remains of a crumbling fortress. Though the "fortress" is nearly abstract and the nude girl merely a pale shadow among sharp lines and jagged shapes, *#25* is a metaphor for the entropic deterioration of the monuments (and girls) so vividly depicted in the earliest paintings in the series. Compare this with paintings from Kellogg's Arbor series, in which skeletal trees seem to yearn for foliage, thirsting in a Beckettian nightmare for life where there is none. Desolation and dissolution are here depicted through Cubist reduction and portend Kellogg's tragic and dark later years.

Wiley Cox

American, 1885–1960

The Shed, 1940

Dollhouse from the Kendall Seagrave Memorial Dollhouse Collection
Gift of the Ambrose J. and Vivian T. Seagrave Family Trust

The Shed was constructed by Vivian Seagrave's brother and amateur artist, Uncle Wiley, and presented to Kendall on her eighth birthday. Though Cox was rarely invited to the estate because of his "woodsy" character, he was said to have been Kendall's favorite uncle. She enthusiastically accepted this strange dollhouse, which amounts to little more than a few shoddy rooms covered with a thatch roof. Uncle Wiley told Kendall that he had met a witch in a similar, life-sized structure, and that she let him use the building as a base of operations for long expeditions into the mountains, where he hunted for owlbears, an imaginary owl/bear hybrid he insisted thrived in the thick forests around the Seagrave's country manor and the northeastern United States. Though Cox was no craftsman, one can still admire the rustic charm of the hand-hewn furniture, accessories, and the dolls. One is a long-bearded Uncle Wiley sitting on the lap of a witch, naked but for her pointy hat.

At times she feels as if her body is hardening, her joints seizing as if she will soon wake unable to move. Every morning she wills herself out of bed, wills herself downstairs to the kitchen, moving through the stiffness until she is mobile. Today, with each step, she feels her cartilage wearing away, her muscles mineralizing.

At night she looks up at the ceiling in the light of the moon coming through the windows and imagines it is her last night; the memories she has suppressed quiver as she attempts to empty her mind, returning to her breath, shallow and slow. Sometimes the images are too much, pushing, clawing their way forward. No matter how she focuses, she cannot shake them, and even now, standing in front of this model, she cannot stop them.

What the final breath will feel like: slow, long, and deliberate. She will get the most out of her final sensation before she fossilizes. She does not want to die in her sleep; she wants to face death, feel it all, savor her last memory, and then finally, silence. She hopes there is nothing after—she wants nothing more than to no longer exist, her point of view extracted from the world. Gone, nothing can be recorded, nothing accumulated. She will become stone, a statue, and then dust.

At the end, her husband had been afraid. Her face above his face, she saw that his eyes knew, his body knew, and yet, he would not accept it, could not be present and at peace. What a waste.

That is not how it happened; when she looked into his eyes, he had already died. She was not the last thing he saw, not even close. For him, there was only darkness.

A man and a woman, barely thirty—though she does not know for certain, everyone is young to her—walk slowly through the gallery. They are there together, but they stand an awkward distance apart. Maybe they are on a first date, maybe the third, but they both look like they wish they could be anywhere but in the museum while at the same time wanting to seem engaged for the other's sake. She points at a detail. He nods. He stands longer than usual in front of one painting, tells her something about it, and she agrees.

She wants them to touch one another, to hold hands, for their shoulders to brush lightly. She wants them to look at something together and both *see*, to look and come together.

The shed is the crudest dollhouse in the museum, roughly fashioned and slapped together. The amateur details are crusted with dust, the crevices neglected, the seams between the pieces coming apart. She can see the glue like silken webs barely holding the model together. Why is this piece, unlike all the others here, so neglected? Possibly because it is less art and more artifact. As an individual work, it is both awful and terrifying, the Uncle Wiley doll crude and stained, sitting on the yellowy nude. She can't fathom its importance, the justification for the space it takes in the gallery. More broadly, she is puzzled by much of the museum, this confusion of pieces in a seemingly random array.

The geography of the space, the layout of the galleries, and the order of the works could be a message, she supposes, a secret code for some visitor to read and decipher. She laughs, cannot comprehend such a purpose. She is limited by what she sees, able to attend to only what draws her to it.

Squire John Ensign
American, 1865–1970

Hypoxia, 1970
Oil on panel

Completed just before Ensign's death from a shattered heart, *Hypoxia* is rare in that it does not depict trains or anything associated with railroading. The painting is also unusual in being one of only a handful of abstract paintings by Ensign, whose forays into that style were as mediocre as his vast catalog of realist paintings. In examining the frayed threads of black, ocher, and rust, one can imagine Ensign's oxygen-deprived blood, the color and viscosity of maple syrup, barely moving through arteries and veins as brittle as dry twigs, his frangible heart softly throbbing as it strained to feed his withered hands so that he could push a brush across this slick panel one last time.

Frank Coin
American, 1915–1992

Untitled #15, 1965
Graphite on paper

By the early 1960s, Coin had shunned Cubism, a long overdue stylistic shift. Critics, once inexplicably excited by Coin's endless Braque "homages," by then, like the public and surely Coin himself, had grown weary of twenty-five years of derivative geometrical planes. With *Untitled #15*, Coin's vocabulary shifted. Though still geometric, his style turned toward the minimal and the spiritual in the form of delightfully, if fussily, precise lines arranged in a great cosmic grid—an exciting shift, to say the least, though one wonders if anybody's life would be any different had he stopped at *Untitled #10*.

In 1970, Coin emigrated from the United States to rural Ontario, where he continued to explore symmetry. In photographs, he can be seen with a young Iris Babbitt, with whom he was rumored to have had a long affair. What she saw in him or his work, I do not know.

Roscoe Crooks (born Matthew Peuse)
American, 1930–2005

Corral, 1981
Oil on canvas

Though Western themes had fallen largely out of fashion, Crooks clung to both the genre and to critical acclaim among enthusiasts. In *Corral*, we see a work exploring typical subjects at the height of his interest in replicating the washed out burnt oranges, yellows, and browns of the Old American West. Crooks uses clichéd tropes to evoke a sense of nostalgia. However, the deep wrinkles on the cowboys' stone faces, their thick biceps, shredded clothing, and the skeletal horses around which they gather betray a different reality.

My education as an art historian was often questioned when the museum trustees still cared about such things; specifically, they wondered why we needed even a single Crooks oil. Upon being promoted to curator after most of the museum employees had moved on and no qualified replacement could be convinced of the merits of this museum, I announced my sovereignty by purchasing this, a second Crooks, and later a third, one of many questionable acquisitions.

Iris Babbitt

American, 1940–2007

Ghost, 1975

Oil on canvas

Perhaps the most traditional of Babbitt's paintings on display here, *Ghost* relies solely on typical materials—oil paint and canvas—and the subject matter, a Victorian parlor, is unusual for the artist. The title prompts most viewers to try to find the ghost in the canvas. Perhaps behind the thick draperies? Or is it Babbitt herself—the unseen artist—who is the ghost? Or perhaps this painting was a premonition. The paranormal investigators I hired to validate the posthumous Babbitt paintings took particular interest in this piece as they scanned the museum for signs of haunting; it was before this piece that they found the most activity, not in the cursed paintings or sculptures, but in this small work, this minor moment in Babbitt's career. The aura around the painting registered in the far infrared on the electromagnetic spectrum, and they noticed a peculiar odor around the frame. Moreover, the air temperature in front of the painting is .5 degrees Fahrenheit lower than the ambient temperature. One of the investigators claimed he could hear Babbitt calling his name when he held his ear to the painting.

She does not need to be convinced of the reality of ghosts. She knows the ways in which desire and belief can become manifest.

Her husband haunts her; she can push him away, but he lurks in the murky chemistry of her brain, emerging when her guard is down. His spectral form in the doorway suddenly present once again though his body is no longer breathing. A man, maybe her father, appears at the margins of her vision—a distant figure on the horizon—his face almost fully formed, but never distinct, never real.

A mouse scurries across the floor from beneath a bench, pauses to examine some bit, then runs to the wall, where it shimmies through a slim crack. She looks for a guard or someone to inform—this trespasser is surely something they will want to investigate—but she is alone in the gallery. She approaches the wall. The crack is coin-thin, not large enough for a mouse to slide through, but she is certain of what she saw. She wonders what a mouse could survive on here—there is no cafeteria, only the enormous gift shop. Perhaps it feasts on old paint.

She remembers as a child how the apartment she and her mother lived in, the brick duplex, was under constant assault by bats, bats that would appear as if from nowhere in the living room, their bedrooms, once in the bathroom, flapping frantically in chaotic patterns, trying to find a way out. She would seek refuge in her favorite escapes—beneath the bed, in the linen closet, under the dining room table, hidden by the shroud of the table cloth—while her mother chased the bats with a tennis racket and trash can, sometimes for hours, until she could kill or trap the things to release outdoors. Her mother would complain; dispatching bats was a man's job, she'd say, and only at those moments would she lie on the couch, exhausted, with the tennis racket still in her hands and make a plea to no one in particular for somebody to please help her.

She wanted to help her mother, but she never knew how except to do what she was told, though she often felt the kind of misery that children feel when asked to drudge—dishes, dusting, sweeping. In retrospect, her complaints were petty; she was grateful for her mother, did not care about money, but still, she dreamed of dark mansions on hills, trips to the lake, extravagant toys she knew she didn't deserve and could not afford. These were only fantasies.

Her mother had always insisted she was born without a father, a miracle. Her mother said not to tell, that no one should know—but she knows; somehow she knows. She remembers emerging—her birth, no, her rebirth, a child of the cold lake, crawling onto the gravel, exhausted, a ghost appearing from the darkness.

Her childhood haunts her in indistinct impressions, glimpses, and an ache. How can any of it be real, this orphan fantasy? But still, she remembers water.

The function of art, she thinks, is to cause the viewer look outward, to empathize with the rest of the world, but all this looking does is force her back inside, the collisions of memory and fantasy always fighting their way forward. She once cared about many things, but now she finds she has few cares, fewer desires. All she can hope for is equilibrium.

Parker Flint

American, 1935–1970

Portrait, 1957

Oil on canvas

Gift of the Ambrose J. and Vivian T. Seagrave Family Trust

In 1955, Flint took the Seagrave family to court, insisting she was owed a share of the family's fortune due to a provision in the will of Ambrose Seagrave stipulating a small percentage of the estate should be divided among first cousins. Flint forged documents inserting her onto a shadowy branch of the family tree and made her claim, though after finding out that the vast fortune had been severely depleted even before Ambrose's death, aside from the portion locked away in a trust for the founding of this museum, she dropped her case, though still maintained she was a cousin to the family. As a consolation, the trust commissioned her to paint a portrait of the trustees to hang in the museum. Flint was no artist, so rendered the family as crude blobs. We now proudly hang this portrait, by order of the trustees, here in the lobby, the first thing visitors to the museum see. Parker Flint went on to be the first woman to swim from Long Beach, CA, to Catalina Island, though she perished on the beach minutes after completing her record-breaking journey.

Alphonse Fontaine

American, 1920–2001

Roulette, 1965

Oil on canvas

A wisp of light appears to sing across this murky chasm, echoing like a pebble dropping into a subterranean pool. The detritus of my mind rolls across the basin of my brain, ripples, clacks against the inside of my thin and brittle skull like a chick about to hatch. Though I long for it, my trepanist is reluctant to burr a hole through such a frangible veneer, preferring instead to wait for whatever wretch grows inside to open its husk and expose my cerebral matter to the cleansing air.

Artist Unknown

The Barn, 1940
Dollhouse from the Kendall Seagrave Memorial Dollhouse Collection
Gift of the Ambrose J. and Vivian T. Seagrave Family Trust

Kendall Seagrave was said to hide in the family's barn on many occasions, sometimes sleeping with her beloved thoroughbred, Strong Adhesive, and a tiny goat that lived with the horse. *The Barn* was given to her as a gift on her eighth birthday by the kitchen staff. In addition to containing models of all of her thoroughbred horses, *The Barn* also boasts pigs, a cow, a donkey, a nest of spider monkeys, cats, and a crafty fox—animals Kendall Seagrave herself would never see in person. 1938 was also the year Kendall's father would be indicted for tax evasion stemming from several shell corporations he used to funnel money from illegal trading activities involving the importation and sale of gorilla meat and a scheme to avoid sugar tariffs. He never went to trial, probably in part due to Kendall's death and a series of bribes to high-powered friends. Though some of the fortune survives, thanks to the value of the family's real estate, held by the Seagrave Family Trust, the vast Seagrave fortune diminished quickly after Kendall Seagrave's disappearance. So devastated was Ambrose, he could barely manage his affairs, and though Vivian seemed frugal, she developed a gambling habit, suffering huge losses betting on horse races.

Louis Rocha
American, 1970–

Phoner, 2011
Video, sound, 14 min.

Over the course of six years, the artist painstakingly captured video of people dropping their cell phones into fountains, ponds, rivers, grill fires, deep fryers, and in one case the mouth of a hungry Potomac dolphin. Rocha shot the footage at busy tourist destinations around Washington, D.C., where he would wait until somebody happened to drop their device. The artist claims that he would routinely record as many as one hundred hours before capturing the horror of a dropped phone. The patience required of the artist is as impressive as the film itself, cut to focus on the reactions of the people more than the tragicomic loss of their expensive gadgets.

Viviana van Weenen

American, 1953–2002

Instantly Unrecognizably Identifiable, 2002

Chromogenic prints from digital files [10]

After meditating in a cave in central Pennsylvania for three years, van Weenen traveled by rail across Canada to her home in Seattle, where she began to set fire to the contents of garbage dumpsters, photographing the immolation. While we are lucky to have seen these photographs on display elsewhere, *Instantly Unrecognizably Identifiable* is a series of prints van Weenen made of children she photographed while working at a Sears Portrait Studio. Though for the sake of her job she would shake a toy above her head and promise candy in order to make the children smile, the prints she made for herself were of the scowling, ungrateful children as they were, without stimulation or reward.

The boy with the wet hands reappears, standing below the row of photographs, the top of his head barely reaching the bottom of the prints. He leans his shoulder against the white wall, looks maniacally above him. A thick strand of saliva hangs from his bottom lip.

She wonders if she should say something, ask him if he is lost. He doesn't belong here.

His blue-and-white striped shirt is smudged from the right shoulder to the hem with something brownish black, like a fudgsicle melted over him. His hair a mess, he looks like he has been through something serious in the moments since she last saw him. Still, he is without parents, and the room is empty except for the two of them. Though she feels some responsibility as an adult, her age excuses her from taking action. She doesn't know what this boy desires, what he is capable of.

She feels a kinship with orphans, but has no sympathy for this child.

A man in a long coat—an expensive coat, soft black wool—walks into the gallery, removes a painting hidden inside his coat, and leans it against the wall. He is wearing a knit hat pulled low over his forehead, sunglasses, and his is jaw obscured by a white beard. Removing the Fontaine, he sets it carefully next to the other painting before replacing the original with the one he brought in with him—a seemingly identical copy. He lifts the Fontaine from the floor, holds it against his chest, closes his coat, and walks calmly and confidently toward the exit.

She looks around the gallery for someone to deal with this—she is in no position to stop him, and the boy seems oblivious, only interested in the photographs above him. She could go to the entrance, find somebody to tell, but she is tired; the new Fontaine seems as good as the old. In the center of the gallery are two worn leather couches back to back. She sits and sinks, wonders if she will be able to stand again; if she is stuck, will there be anyone to help her?

The boy has stuffed his hand into his mouth again, all the way to his wrist. He's practiced this feat, grotesque and astounding. His eyes are proud as his face reddens. He bends forward as if he is about to expel something from his stomach, retching to eject his hand, now coated with skeins of slobber. He takes a deep breath, belches, and laughs; he lifts his hand to the photograph above, extends his fingers, and plants his hand firmly on the print, dragging it down, leaving a viscous streak, the smear glistening in the light.

She tries to stand but is trapped in the cavern of the couch. The cracks in the leather exude the sweat of old bodies, the smell intense and nauseating. She tries again, thrusting with force, the momentum allowing her to stand. She feels drained, her head suddenly numb. Without something to steady her, she wobbles in place, extending her arms for balance. She manages to not fall back into the couch, instead stumbling forward, nearly toppling. The blood returns to her brain, and she finds equilibrium; she straightens her coat, looks again for somebody, anybody, who might have helped her. The boy stands below his creation, the saliva still dripping from the photograph. He stares at her, pushing his hand back into his mouth as if to say *You are next*.

Cody Thorn

American, 1955–1995

Tart Biters, 1985

Acrylic, sand, wheelbarrow, found materials, plywood

Prior to achieving fame for his monumental minimalist sculpture, Thorn lived in Mexico City, where, influenced by Rauschenberg and Duchamp, he created close to a hundred pieces from found objects. Similar to Rauschenberg's *Combines*, Thorn's *Assemblages* achieve a level of grit and spirit that set his work apart from that of his contemporaries and forebears. Thorn here emphasizes orderly geometric patterns—perhaps to suggest the grid of his adopted home of Mexico City—while preserving a sense of chaos and chance in the seemingly random selection of objects. The tufts of wild animal fur serve two purposes. While they disguise the uneven seams between the objects, they also suggest the presence of the *bestial* in the detritus left by humans. Though all the pieces are recognizable castoffs of an urban environment—building sand, a wheelbarrow, plywood—the fur suggests the remains of something inhuman: something unrestrained, instinctual, has touched these objects.

Iris Babbitt

American, 1940–2007

Typographic, 2005

Acrylic, latex housepaint on drywall

Oh, Iris, how you drift down my dark halls like an afterimage! Every day you fade as if even in death you cannot escape illness. Your afterlife is just another death. I see you for a moment, and I speak to you, but you are no longer there.

Alan Frutices
American, 1880 [reported]-2010

Healthy Harvest, 1940
Oil on canvas

A bowl of ripe fruit—three bananas, two apples, a pear, a pineapple, a mangosteen—and three human hearts are centered on a dirty butcher block in this meticulous still life. Frutices' most famous painting, *Breakfast Eels*, caused a ripple of shock through the art world, not because of what it depicted, but because of its horrible smell. *Healthy Harvest*, painted three years later, also raised brows, not because of its odor—this one smells fine—but because of viewers' distaste for the display of appealing fruit so near to human organs. Frutices, who claimed to be 130 years old as he neared death in 2010, regularly dined on the hearts of goats and eels, while eating "five servings of fruit and five servings of vegetables" every day. He claimed he would live forever, stipulating in his will that on the off chance he should die he was not be embalmed and was to be periodically disinterred so as not to be trapped underground in the likely event of his resurrection.

Gaylord Kellogg
American, 1891–1937

Nude Girl in Fragmented Light #2, 1920
Oil on canvas

Before tragedy would befall the artist and his family in 1927, Kellogg spent years working on a series of impressionistic portraits of nude girls in near darkness. In the late works of the series, the paintings verged on the abstract, so much so that the girls would be difficult to identify without the titles. In this early example, however, the figure is clearly visible, if not well defined. Though one might question Kellogg's obsession with painting [and obscuring] naked girls, one could also applaud his problematizing taboo subjects. Were the girls to be painted photorealistically, they would be overtly sexualized, but because the figures are indistinct, even in the early examples, the viewer is put in the uncomfortable position of imagining the girl. It is notable here that the subject of *Nude Girl in Fragmented Light #2* is set, not in a remote crumbling fortress, but rather a public place, a café, where she is surrounded by begging feral cats.

Dorothy Phelps
American, 1927–

Barn Owls, 1980
Oil on Masonite

As one of the most celebrated paintings in the museum, *Barn Owls* is a magnet for visitors, who love to photograph themselves in front of it to convey to their internet friends that they spend their free time engaging in pursuit of cultural literacy by visiting obscure regional American art museums in second-tier cities, museums whose collections are far from magnificent, museums that have, with meager budgets, cobbled together some representative collection of minor works by unknown artists.

Are you stimulated by this painting? Does it move you? What moves you? Does the yellow glow from the stark office buildings remind you of the eyes of an owlbear in a concrete forest? What do you see in the eyes?

In an audio interview conducted with Phelps in 2014, the artist claimed she was interested in metaphor and how her highly symbolic renderings of urban commercial spaces might say something about humanity's twisted relationship with nature, how in carving out a place for ourselves, we have pushed away from the natural world instead of toward it. In *Barn Owls*, one can see this symbolism in the lack of green space, the lack of natural light, and the murky night sky, but really?

Rowena Copperpot
American, 1887–1945

The Grandest Illusion, 1940
Oil on canvas
Gift of the Ambrose J. and Vivian T. Seagrave Family Trust

Commissioned by the Seagrave family, *The Grandest Illusion* depicts Kendall Seagrave in the months before her disappearance. Can we really say she *disappeared*? How likely is it that she swam to safety during such a storm, even wearing a life preserver? And where did she go if she made it to shore? Did she start a new life, one away from her life at the Seagrave estate? Perhaps the biggest question is why she disappeared at all—if it was an accident, if she was pushed, or if some hidden horror compelled her to jump. Perhaps there is a hint in the title of the painting, which suggests that Copperpot recognized something behind the happy façade of Kendall's smiling face.

Ultimately, however, there are no answers. Kendall Seagrave is at the bottom of Lake Ontario with a few of her dolls and the body of the painter Jillian Waterstone, Hans Osterhagen's estranged lover, who also *disappeared* that stormy day. Though Osterhagen was on the boat, he was very drunk, as were the dozen other artists and hangers-on, including Wiley Cox, and though noone saw exactly what happened, the shadow over Osterhagen lasted for months until he was finally acquitted. It's unclear why the Seagrave family forgave him and subsequently made him welcome at the estate, where he became a fixture. Copperpot's *The Grandest Illusion* is said to be one of the most accurate portraits of the girl while still being flattering.

Tanya Conn

American, 1931–2001

Obtusion, 1954

Watercolor on paper

In my twenties, I suffered from what is known as rabbit starvation from eating nothing but game for forty-five days on a spiritual journey I took in the Uinta Mountains in northern Utah. For weeks I craved nothing but bread, pasta, and the fattiest beef while subsisting on rabbits and bits of a rotting elk. Near the end of my journey, sick and weak, I consumed a handful of berries and, supine on the surface of a rock, stared into the sky and hallucinated for seventy-two hours. I cannot adequately describe what I saw, but it is close enough to Conn's impressionistic watercolor depicting the collapse of a mineshaft on a family of mule deer that I am chilled and shivery whenever I look upon it.

Prints of *Obtusion* are available in the gift shop, in addition to coffee mugs, tie clasps, and silk scarves inspired by the painting.

She stands before this strange painting, not yet ready to go, though she does not know why. The billowing colors circulate in chaos, the arcs of paint slowly spiraling inward. She can't visualize the mineshaft or mule deer in the seemingly disordered mess; instead, the movement of the layered hues sedates her. She stares.

Something heavy drops on the floor in another gallery and bounces, like a bowling ball has fallen from the ceiling. Startled, she looks up, takes a step back. How long has she been looking?

The boy has disappeared. A small guard leans against the wall in the archway between galleries, his eyes hidden by reflective sunglasses. His leg is bent, his foot resting against the arch behind him. A frayed toothpick hangs from his lips. She can smell his cologne, bright and floral.

She approaches him. "Do you work here?"

His uniform jacket is two sizes too big, and the tails of his long shirt, stuffed into tight pants, bunch over his thighs. She cannot recall museum guards wearing police uniforms. A badge in the shape of a star hangs limply from his breast pocket, and though he has a holster on his belt, there is no gun. The uniform looks more like a Halloween costume: the badge some kind of coated plastic, the veneer worn and chipped.

"No." He stares through her.

The young cannot imagine their own transformation. She is old, yes, but her mind is the same as it has always been, though bloated with memory. For a moment, she thinks the guard will be lucky to live as long as she, but then revises—she does not wish old age on anyone.

"I think somebody stole a painting," she says. "And a boy defaced a photograph. I can't find anybody."

"I can't help you," he says. "I don't work here." He kicks himself away from the wall, tips his hat to her, and walks away.

Obedience Bradstreet
American, 1845–1923

The Cathedral, 1908
Dollhouse from the Kendall Seagrave Memorial Dollhouse Collection
Gift of the Ambrose J. and Vivian T. Seagrave Family Trust

Crafted by celebrated dollhouse builder Obedience Bradstreet in 1908, *The Cathedral* is one of the grandest miniature cathedrals of the Edwardian Miniature Cathedral Renaissance. While the Seagrave family rarely attended church for security reasons, Kendall often sought refuge by escaping, metaphorically, into this enormous model, situating a doll likeness of herself, clad in a gray cloak to conceal her identity, in the back pews while a doll priest recited his sermon. *The Cathedral* is of course incredible in its scale, but equally impressive are the hand-sewn parishioners filling every pew. While Bradstreet was renowned for her craftsmanship and architectural eye, she was also a fine doll maker. Each congregant's head was modeled, bisque-fired, and hand-painted by the artist.

Vivian Seagrave's brother, Wiley Cox, a documented agalmatophiliac and noted statuary collector, purchased *The Cathedral*.

Squire John Ensign
American, 1865–1970

Magnificent America, 1935
Oil on canvas

The key to this painting is the bright edge of the clouds at the top of the canvas, kissed by sunshine like God's lips resting on the wings of an angel. Notice the changing light over the length of the preposterously long canvas, how the sun fades slowly to gray, then black, then blacker still until we reach the faces of the magnificent workers, so monstrous and large we dare not get too close for fear of getting in their way. Oh, manufacturing! Oh, factories! Dirt and broken workers shadowed by a gossamer film of soot! I hear America singing her varied carols!

Sandra Wallace
American, 1980–

Nautical Disasters, 2009
New media

Wallace created approximately three hundred animated GIFs—appropriated from internet videos showing boats and ships sinking, exploding, and catching on fire—for *Nautical Disasters*, which displays one hundred rotating, randomly selected animations. *Nautical Disasters* comments on the twenty-first century obsession with disaster, its twenty-four-hour news and surveillance, and its constant, overburdening physical and digital violence. Despite the staccato onslaught of looping destruction, many viewers find the images cathartic and even soothing—happy to see something that feels to them like the internet hanging on a giant screen in an art museum—and can be found staring into the healing light, sometimes for hours.

Iris Babbitt

American, 1940–2007

Barn Storm, 1964

Oil on panel

Once, in the early phase of our relationship, Babbitt and I sat together in the parlor and flipped through magazines. She had an unending appetite for celebrity gossip rags, especially *Us Weekly*. I was glad to supply her with them—anything to make her afterlife as comfortable as it could be. Babbitt often asked me to cook for her. She missed eating but could still smell things, and the waft of savory stew comforted her endless emptiness, so I happily learned new and interesting recipes while she hovered nearby.

From her chair in the parlor, I could see Babbitt was distracted. I asked if she wanted me to turn the page for her (though she could usually do this herself, it sometimes was too much), and when she said no, I asked what was bothering her. She told me she thought that perhaps she wasn't a ghost at all, that she was really dead, the kind of dead where the soul dies too, and that perhaps her very existence was due to my imagination and obsession, an obsession she noted was both unusual and creepy. She said she'd never believed in ghosts, and that while there was pleasure in being just a little bit alive—she felt lucky—she couldn't help but think that this was all in my head. I told her if that were true—if she was all in my head—it would mean that I was creating the doubts she was feeling, and since I had no doubt she was real, the fact that she doubted her own existence was actually proof of it. This consoled her, but still I wondered if she was right.

She often told me to keep our relationship a secret, because if my colleagues found out, I would be ruined. I didn't want to hide anything. I loved her and didn't care how strange or unbelievable it was to others; sadly, I knew what she said was true, though all of my colleagues had resigned or been laid off.

Barn Storm is an exemplary early work, done while Babbitt was still shedding the last tufts of her teachers' influence. The nod to Pop Art is obvious, but interesting only because of how quickly she abandoned pop elements in the work that would immediately follow *Barn Storm*. Some argue that her interest in collage—a primary tool in almost all of her post-1965 work—came from Pop Art, but in fact her influences were much wider. In the shattered depictions of iconic images of 1950s housewives, *Barn Storm* suggests the coming turbulence of the late '60s, as well as the changing role of women.

Dolores Lababera
American, 1945–1976

Elephants, 1957
Watercolor on paper
Gift of the Ambrose J. and Vivian T. Seagrave Family Trust

One of the most profound criticisms of contemporary art and Abstract Expressionism is some variant of "my child could have done that." The statement often sparks a dialectical investigation into the role of the artist, the meaning of art, the challenges of abstraction, and the ontological quest. All of these ideas were covered in one of my mail-order courses, though I have long forgotten what was discussed.

As a twelve-year-old, Lababera smeared brown and blue watercolor onto paper, framed it, and sold it to the Seagrave Family Trust, troubling the notion that children cannot create works of genius, for in *Elephants*, everything is contained—the history of Western art, the answer to what it means to be human, to live, and to die.

Chester Cornwallis
American, 1847–1907

A Trip to the Moon, 1905
Oil on canvas

A strange vision of what Cornwallis imagined would be on the moon were we to someday visit it, *A Trip to the Moon* very accurately predicted what the Apollo 11 lunar module would look like, what the astronauts would be wearing, and the general color and landscape of Earth's satellite. Beyond Cornwallis's prescience, what is peculiar about this painting is the anger it evokes in those who see it—so much so that the canvas has been attacked by mad patrons over a dozen times. Specifically, *A Trip to the Moon* has been stabbed and slashed three times, shot twice, and set on fire once.

The painting is now shielded behind bullet- and shatterproof glass. Please take care not to step or reach beyond the rope, no matter how provoking the image.

Should you wish to attack a copy of *A Trip to the Moon*, prints are on sale in the gift shop.

Landers Dingle
American, 1905–1990

The Statue Cleaner, 1985
Oil on canvas

A maintenance worker of heroic proportions wraps his body around an enormous marble statue, polishing the legs of Saint Sebastian, tethered to a dead stone tree and riddled with stone arrows. The worker and statue entwine as if they are one body, their skin one skin, the worker's eyes locked in reverence on the martyr while a sinister imp peeks at the scene from around a corner. Our own museum was long ago cleansed of its goblins using a mixture of sugar and cement set out for the creatures after closing. When asked to dispose of the withered carcasses each morning, I found the task surprisingly satisfying and educational, and it was then that I knew my relationship to the museum would be a long one.

Stella Steven Swayze
American, 1977–

Lunch at Your Desk, 2010
Installation

In the short story "On Exactitude in Science," Argentine writer Jorge Luis Borges describes a fictional map of the world that had "the scale of a mile to the mile." In this large installation, Swayze asks the question *what if that scale were reversed*? The magnitude of this work—so large as to warrant its own room in a museum already wanting for space—belies its importance, though the project pleasantly reminds me of my master's degree examination, in which one of my advisors asked me to conceive of and describe a museum designed for dogs.

Artist Unknown

The Conservatory, ~1920s

Dollhouse from the Kendall Seagrave Memorial Dollhouse Collection
Gift of the Ambrose J. and Vivian T. Seagrave Family Trust

Kendall Seagrave's dolls spent hours in *The Conservatory*, where they loved to hear the rain hitting the glass octagonal dome. In the winter, they sat on the benches beneath the banana trees in the tropical warmth and read their favorite books. In the summer, when the louvered windows were open and the breeze blew through the lush foliage [exquisitely modeled in miniature by arborists, topiarists, and gardeners], the dolls would gather for parties, eating tiny cakes and drinking tiny glasses of lemonade. In the Seagrave Estate's larger version of this dollhouse, Kendall would hide in the bushes with her own books and spy on Vivian Seagrave and the artist Hans Osterhagen, who, while Ambrose was away visiting his vast network of beaver furriers, would languish for hours, naked and entwined beneath a sea mango tree.

She can hear the sound of rain on glass; she sits on a bench, looks up at the rivulets cascading down from the top peak of the conservatory, the sky outside thick and gray. The air inside is always humid, always summer. She ducks beneath the waxy green leaves of some monstrous plant and listens.

The muffled sound of boots in mud: footsteps in the dormant garden outside. Rain leaks through the glass ceiling, falls into a bucket on the brick path. The water in the bucket has reached the top and threatens to spill over. She holds her breath and listens to the sound of her body. She can feel her faint pulse. She listens to herself exhale when she can no longer bear not to breathe.

Hands wipe the water away from the conservatory windows. A man in a drenched suit looks in, his face obscured by a feathery mask. She has seen him before, knows those black eyes even though his face is hidden.

Sometimes she smells something—something burnt, a mix of coffee and rye. Sometimes the smell buries something else—an herbal cologne, like tea. Sometimes the smell reminds her of something she has known before—something close and warm, pressed against her. Something catches in her brain for a moment then escapes; sometimes she works to bring it forward, other times allows herself to drift.

A man lifts a thermos to his lips; he is watching her, she knows, though his eyes fall on the dollhouse. He stinks of coffee and cigarettes; she can smell it lifting from his yellow skin, from his wet coat. His breaths are long and labored, his aura a long wheeze. Does he see what she sees?

She summons memories from half-thoughts and fragments, stitching together images.

She does not remember her childhood, really, only things she'd read in books, pictures she'd seen. A recurring dream, swimming in a cold lake, exhaustion, her mouth full of water. A drowning fantasy: killing herself, rebirth.

Hovering over her sleeping husband on the night of his death, counting his breaths. She had gone for a long walk alone that night, walked to the edge of the neighborhood to a narrow path into the woods. Wet leaves beneath her feet, churning up the smell of rotten earth. Dusk phantoms gliding between the gnarled trees.

Running down a long hall. Her mother telling her to be quiet, the neighbors sleeping downstairs. She remembers standing in the dark doorway of one of the guest rooms, listening to the party in the ballroom at the end of the hall, wondering where she would hide when the last of the guests left. Sitting at the counter at her mother's restaurant, flipping through a book of photographs of staircases and chandeliers and grand sepia gardens. The shining eyes of a deer in the darkened woods. A crowded boat, the wind and rain.

Augustina Thompson
American, 1934–

The Jerk, 1960
Oil on canvas

The soda jerk serves his customers, happily filling their empty glasses with frothy Coke and scoops of vanilla ice cream. Betsy likes hers with a splash of sarsaparilla, and Donald likes his creamy and wet. He will order a hot dog after. He'll put the hot dog in his mouth and playfully touch Betsy's leg. She'll suck on her straw and move his hand up her thigh and let him linger there before pushing him away. She'll agree they should go for a drive after their snack. Gertie looks on, standing in front of a tall white canvas-like wall. The light from the diner window highlights her, as if she is on stage, or in a gallery, and though jealous of Betsy and Donald, she is the center here, statuesque and bronzy.

Iris Babbitt

American, 1940–2007

Tectonics, 1994

Clay, metal, twine, sheetrock, PVC

Before Babbitt retreated to my attic to haunt me like a regular ghost, I persuaded her to produce new artwork through me. She resisted. She didn't want to create more work; she had said what she'd wanted to say during her lifetime, and none of it had mattered. Yes, some people liked what she'd done, but she wasn't important. She'd made her peace with that.

But had she? I asked myself. Ghosts had unfinished business—something left to say—and maybe creating new work would give her peace. Of course, I didn't want her to find peace, because she would leave and I was in love!—but greater than my love was my desire to be inhabited, to feel her hand moving through my hand, to *be her*, if only for a few moments, even if it meant the end of our relationship.

A few weeks later, she brought up the idea of making more art, though she was still unsure. She'd clearly been thinking about the possibilities. She told me she couldn't invade my body in such a manner—that possessing the cats or one of the Dachshunds, even, was too much; she hadn't the energy to inhabit me. I told her she could try, just to see if it might work, if she had the stamina, if only for a moment, and in this way we began.

After some practice she found she could easily possess me—perhaps it was my willingness. She created six posthumous works over the course of a year in several minutes-long sessions. This is not one of those works. Nobody takes the ghost pieces seriously yet, though I am confident that once done with their investigations, the group of independent paranormal detectives I have hired will show compelling evidence that Babbitt and I were in fact intimate and that she was able, like an incubus, to take over my body.

Is the work we created by Babbitt, or must we attribute them to some new thing, something that is both of us? Or are we simply to ascribe them to Babbitt's ghost and her spirit's energy and determination to finish something she was unable to finish because of death? Maybe this is simply a new phase in her career, one untethered from the commercial art world or Babbitt's material needs, a world of pure desire and production.

Perhaps it is also some small part of my ongoing war with the museum trustees, who seem to have given up on or forgotten me.

Compared with her posthumous work, *Tectonics* is not impressive. Notice the haphazard construction and the piece's dullness. It is undoubtedly a Babbitt, but it is a terrible example, one she was embarrassed about [she told me], and one she would prefer to be destroyed. But once one's work enters the world, one has no say over such things. I will not destroy it—if Babbitt wants it gone, she will have to do it herself, or possess somebody to do it for her, perhaps a guard or one of our elderly docents.

Roy Butterfield

American, 1945–1991

Blue Matter, 1973

Encaustic on newspaper over canvas

The texture of Butterfield's *Blue Matter* seems to extend well beyond the surface of the canvas, as if the image is trying to stretch into the world. But what does the image mediate with its thick waxen vortex, at once appearing to tunnel into the wall behind it even as it extends away from it? Butterfield explained that the work of this period, like that of other artists exploring nonrepresentational art, was about the *material*. "These aren't pictures of anything in the way that you want them to be pictures of something," he said. "I'm not trying to capture God or heaven or the ocean bottom here. To describe this thing at all is a waste of your time. It's beeswax over some newspapers." If you look closely, you can read a few newspaper headlines below the surface of the colored wax. What could they mean?

Gordy Franklin

American, 1970–2010

Erection, 1999

Bronze

Franklin's *Erection* could be a metaphor for the art world, ironic or not, though few would describe Franklin as subtle. The luster of the medium destroys the verisimilitude of the otherwise painstakingly realistic sculpture. One might guess that Franklin, who was killed by a shark, imagined not his own erection when casting this piece but some unrealized ideal that could only exist as simulacrum.

Archie Ansell

American, 1897–1965

Catastrophe, 1940

Oil on canvas

Though not officially affiliated with the Surrealists, Ansell's dream landscapes owe a hefty debt to the group. *Catastrophe* demonstrates a glimmer of originality by eschewing melting objects, chessboards, and ants for this competent panorama of ballet-dancing squids. The effect of the mildly surprising juxtaposition is not alienation or psychological torment; instead, the painting induces laughter in the connoisseurs of mediocrity who frequent this museum. *Catastrophe* is indisputably ordinary, but is an affordable representation of a major artistic movement that we would be uncomfortable disregarding.

Shahd Amari
American, 1980–

Somnambulance, 2012
Metal, plastic, fluorescent light installation

To enter this gallery is to enter a spiral of light so pure, so white, one must look at the ground lest one go blind. Perhaps that is an exaggeration. *Somnambulance* will not literally blind you, though the experience of it is one of looking away from the thing itself, art that compels you to retreat, the only respite from the maddening brightness: the act of walking away.

She closes her eyes and waits. The flood of light leaks through the thin red membrane of her eyelids. How she must look like a wisp of the woman she once was, like a ghost, nearly invisible in the blinding glare.

She begins to feel her heart in the stillness of the room. She can hear the buzzing hum of the fluorescents, but it is as if the intense brightness has devoured all sound, the other senses submitting to the intense bombardment of one.

What must be reconciled before she goes? Her family? Her estate? She leaves very little—her husband's niece, a pittance in a blind trust. What's left—what she'd acquired, what he'd left her—distributed to a few friends, more acquaintances than intimates. She knows no one will miss her; no one will care. The small parting gifts are like payments; somebody should attend her funeral, even if they are there only out of obligation.

As she stands in the empty light, she realizes she is the only thing to behold in the brightness of the installation. At the end, she has become the subject of the work, a pastiche of experience and reinvention, the object of the viewer's gaze, should they choose to look.

Her kneecaps burn. She's been standing too long, sitting too long. It is time to lie down, to look up at the ceiling, searching for silence in the void of the smooth white plaster.

Kelly Constance Beal

American, 1921–1991

The Grave Diggers, 1949

Oil on panel

One of the few female army doctors to serve in World War II, Beal became known for her paintings of atrocity. *The Grave Diggers* is among her more somber works; the title is clearly metaphorical, suggesting with its depiction of nurses treating amputees that these soldiers will not last long. Painted in the style of Vermeer and other seventeenth-century Dutch masters, the hospital room is claustrophobic and domestic. Notice the faces of the women treating the wounded, how they are turned away from the brutalized bodies, angled toward the sliver of light coming from the slim window above them. The painting on the wall of the hospital, a glorious Napoleonic battle scene in splendid color, contradicts the reality of Beal's subjects. The odd cockleshells on the floor on the lower right side of the canvas, next to a pair of empty boots, hint at the fleeting nature of life, but also repressed sexuality.

Artist Unknown

The Chateau, ~1920s

Dollhouse from the Kendall Seagrave Memorial Dollhouse Collection
Gift of the Ambrose J. and Vivian T. Seagrave Family Trust

Kendall Seagrave's dolls experienced their darkest moments in *The Chateau*, a cold, vast model purchased for Kendall by her mother from an Estonian prince. Attached to the drawing room on the ground floor is a cramped, windowless chamber with only a small worktable, a chair, and a fainting couch. On the wall of the room is a portrait of the Estonian prince and his greyhounds. Kendall would often send her favorite doll here after rescuing her from the labyrinth or after an afternoon in the conservatory, and she would weep quietly on the fainting couch or write in her diary. After Kendall's death, the doll's diary was examined for clues; however, authorities found the tiny notebook to be inscribed with glyphs belonging to an unknown language, a language perhaps familiar only to Kendall and her dolls. Though the original still sits on the desk in the chamber in *The Chateau*, facsimiles of the diary are for sale in the gift shop.

Daniel Cortez
American, 1930–

The Contortionists, 1951
Oil on canvas

Imagine Cortez's long brush, gooey with paint, gyrating against the canvas. *The Contortionists* transports us to our deepest fantasies—an unusually heavy meal, decadent creams and cheeses, spider sex and the rampant deforestation of a pristine, virginal wood.

Wilma Scales
American, 1924–1988

After and Everything, 1957
Oil pastel on cardboard

The finest mouths in the museum, buttery and true, like night crawlers, grace the faces of these children. Their eyes, like the icy water of a swimming hole, rivet into you, and their jagged ribs take you to the rusted railroad trellis you walked as a child on your way to the forest where you and your chums lathered yourselves in camphor and lay naked in a secret glen. You can taste the blood on these boys' cheeks, smell their fetid hair, feel the sharp gravel cutting their bony feet, and your memories become their memories.

Aprons and kites inspired by *After and Everything* are available in the gift shop.

Iris Babbitt

American, 1940–2007

Celibacy Machine, 1978

Polaroids on board, oil, rubber cement, razor blades

Babbitt once mistook me for her first love. The relationship hadn't ended well, so she sought revenge on me by possessing my body in anger, chilling me so completely and thoroughly I will never be warm again, never be comfortable.

I don't mind; I can barely remember how it felt to live in my body before. She apologized—she knows it is difficult to be mistaken for a fifty-years-passed lover—but I am not hurt, at least not emotionally; I've come to understand how difficult it is for a ghost to remember details.

We do what we can, though, to remember the best days. I show her the notes I make about our time together and caress the air where her body would be to show her how much I care, how little it means that she's no longer corporeal, how a spirit can sometimes be enough.

Squire John Ensign
American, 1865–1970

Journey of a Lifetime, 1906
Oil on canvas

In this painting, another in Ensign's series of railroad scenes, a family of five—a mother and her four young children—stand on the platform with their luggage, waiting to board the westbound Broadway Limited in Altoona, Pennsylvania. Though not explicit in the painting, the missing father, the date of the painting, and the morose looks affected by all but the youngest child, who appears giddy with excitement, suggest this is the family of the deceased railroad worker in *Common Labor*, here taking advantage of their lifetime passes to travel to Chicago.

Viviana van Weenen
American, 1953–2002

Metaphorism, 2001
Chromogenic print from digital

Viviana van Weenen built the structure depicted in the photograph, a labyrinth of swollen bark and tumescent lumber from diseased trees, in the northwestern Utah desert while hallucinating after surviving on the spoiled carcasses of birds she found along the shores of the Great Salt Lake. I too have eaten rotted birds, and afterward saw visions of bright blue light emitting from floating spheres. Luminous waves frothed from my mouth and bathed my body and transformed my skin into leather. I took hold of the wing of a cloudless sulphur and flew above the city and saw for the first time art, visions twisted and mutilated. The ruins pictured in *Metaphorism*, though partially consumed by the hungry desert, can still be seen at the site, and this photograph, taken by van Weenen before she transmogrified into an enormous fly, flew toward the sun, and was consumed by a snow goose, is the only known record of the project.

Allan Frank, Jr.
American, 1948–

Untitled, 1987
VCT tile and plywood

Most visitors mistake *Untitled* for part of the floor.

Junior Hildebrandt
American, 1860–1947

The Office Tower, 1935
Dollhouse from the Kendall Seagrave Memorial Dollhouse Collection
Gift of the Ambrose J. and Vivian T. Seagrave Family Trust

Inspired by Raymond Hood's late Streamline Moderne/early International Style McGraw-Hill building in New York City, *The Office Tower* is a rare dollhouse in that it replicates, not the home, but the workplace. Here, several floors of steel, green-glazed tiles, and glass are modeled. The interior offices can be accessed from above or by opening any side of the building. The spaces themselves are outfitted with 1930s-era office furniture, typewriters, Telex printers, adding machines, water coolers, and a hand-cranked paper shredder. Though not introduced until 1949, a miniature Xerox Model A xerographic copier is included here because of the model's significant craftsmanship.

On the second floor one finds a dentist's office, with every detail accounted for down to the picks and mirrors used by the dentist, who is here seen hovering over the bloody mouth of a teenaged boy. If you look closely, you can see seven teeth on the dentist's tray.

The horrors of the workplace are evident in the arrangements of the dolls as they go about their labor. A man carrying his belongings in a cardboard box is being escorted out of the building by two security guards. Another man fondles his secretary in the elevator, while another fucks a job candidate in his office at the end of an interview. Another man stabs a coworker with a letter opener in a restroom stall.

The turd-like sculpture in the plaza in front of the office building is a common feature of later midcentury commercial architecture. Though unverified, the miniature glob of cast bronze is attributed to the celebrated outdoor sculptor Catalado Pisano and is the most valuable object in the museum.

Though Kendall Seagrave would never have had to work a day in her life if she had lived, this dollhouse perhaps taught her an important lesson about the dangers of the quotidian world of the modern office, a place from which no one's soul escapes.

Theophilus Harding

American, 1897–1945

Kendall Seagrave, 1945

Oil on canvas

Gift of the Ambrose J. and Vivian T. Seagrave Family Trust

Harding's second portrait of Kendall Seagrave holding a flute is either an enigma, an unfinished work, or a bad metaphor. Kendall had been missing for some years when the Seagrave family commissioned the portrait, so it's difficult to imagine Harding deliberately painted their daughter without a head, though it's possible he meant this decapitaton to evoke her absence. Sadder still, the presence of the flute suggests a music that those who loved her would never hear. Harding was so bad at portraits—he was more of a rocks-and-trees man—that perhaps he couldn't bear to finish the portrait in a way that would look nothing like the missing girl, though it's unlikely after so many years that anybody could really remember what she looked like.

In each painting, a possibility. Every choice runs parallel to the alternatives.

She has wished before to be able to cross that line, to leap across the chasm and join another continuum. She sees her own head on the body of the girl in the painting, a girl who is her and not her—all of these images, what could have been, what *was* in some other history.

A man—older than she, she thinks, though that is surely a miracle if it is true—leans on an umbrella and looks at a painting across the gallery. He's wearing a black raincoat, galoshes, even though she does not remember it raining.

He wears round, wiry glasses, his hair thick and white. He is thin, but not too thin—in shape. Perhaps he will live forever.

She is taken by the idea that he is her husband—not her long dead husband, a man she barely remembers meeting—but another man, a kind man. She remembers walking with him when they were younger, somewhere along the river away from town on an old path. They had probably come from breakfast at the diner after church, walking slowly as a way to preserve the Sunday and the warm sun. They hold hands, he tells her he loves her, and she tells him. She will never leave him, she says, never let him go.

He has been wandering the museum; she feels a great sense of sorrow for forgetting him, but there he is. They'll go home together, where they'll cook dinner, a new recipe she's found; they'll wait for a call from their daughter, who will email new pictures of their granddaughter while they talk. They'll make plans for the holidays even though they're still months away.

"There you are," she says. "I thought I'd forgotten you."

He turns but doesn't seem to recognize her. He smiles. He is kind, but he does not know her.

"I'd like to go home now," she says. "It's been a long day."

As she stares, waiting for his response, he begins to melt away. He turns toward her and starts to speak, but his words slur out of his mouth, down his chin, and onto the floor. As he slowly liquefies, he slides away, like ice on the sidewalk.

"Please, don't go."

She approaches as if to help, but by the time she reaches him, he is gone.

Falco Medina
American, 1936–1983

Mound, 1968
Soil

At night, I relieve myself on this pile.

Annette Morgan

American, 1925–2011

Horseradish Farm, 1972, 1975

Oil on beaverboard

Annette Morgan grew up in Collinsville, IL, the self-proclaimed Horseradish Capital of the World, and in *Horseradish Farm* she commemorates her hometown in this pastoral scene of young, shirtless boys poking their hoes around the thick green foliage of mature horseradish plants. All of Morgan's paintings drip with nostalgia, but it is difficult for even the most naïve Pollyanna to not gag at the cloying sincerity of this one. Notice the earnest faces of the boys, the sweat on their backs, how one boy has raised his arm to wipe his brow with the back of his hand. Notice in the distance the windmill, the silo, the wild dogs, and the hot air balloon floating over the hills (are there hills in Illinois?) while the youngest boy, clearly on the verge of death from heat exhaustion, kneels to capture his friend's urine to drink lest he die from dehydration.

The Horseradish Lover's Cookbook is available in the gift shop.

Curator's Note: It is coincidental that this is the second painting in the museum depicting the cultivation of horseradish.

Iris Babbitt (disputed)
American, 1940–2007

The Ecstatic Geometry, 2012
Acrylic on wood

Though this work's provenance is disputed by all but a few authorities, the evidence presented by an independent team of paranormal investigators and my own knowledge allow me to display the posthumously created Babbitt with confidence. Admittedly, it was my hand that painted *The Ecstatic Geometry* on a cold winter night by the light of the fireplace, but Babbitt's ghost, through me, incontestably executed it. How could it not be so? Note how the style, subject matter, and composition reflect Babbitt's late work. Note the consistency of the color palette. Though crude, the painting is consistent with other posthumous work attributed to her ghost.

Some might argue the piece lacks the artist's skill and vision, but I would remind those who dismiss it that Babbitt produced it as a *ghost*, not a whole person, and it should be expected that her spectral work would not reflect the genius of a living Babbitt. Some say the painting looks like the work of an amateur with barely a scholarly understanding of technique—they note that it is nothing more than a series of smudges, acrylic smeared around a canvas, abstract, but dull and random. I counter those arguments by pointing to the subtle ways the colors blend, the lopsided layout of each swatch, both ordered and chaotic. I point to the abundance of energy in the overlaying of the bright white edges, the way they highlight every shape as if it were illuminated by angelic light.

One might ask *why* Babbitt agreed to create more paintings after her death. I cannot completely answer this question except to say that it was because I loved her, and making these paintings with her was an intimate experience, a gift she gave me while she could, the gift of time.

Gaylord Kellogg
American, 1891–1937

Bald Eagle #13, 1935
Oil on plywood

In *Bald Eagle #13*, the deterioration of Kellogg's health can be seen in the unsteady, almost amateur strokes, here depicting a menacing eagle, wings spread, a family of rats struggling to climb out of its gaping mouth. Like a black hole, the eagle's dark, disproportionately large throat from which the rats scramble seems to open into another world, a world just beyond our reach. If you stare into it long enough, you will be able to glimpse it beyond the darkness.

By 1935 Kellogg's mental health had begun to crumble. Exhausted by depression and nearly incapable of making art, he spent the last two years of his life painting a series of bald eagles in an increasingly abstract, nearly minimal style. After making over a hundred of these paintings, Kellogg died alone wandering the streets of lower Manhattan during a rainstorm.

Bald eagle figurines are available in the gift shop.

Miriam Fox

American, 1947–

Devil's Nightgown, 1970

Oil on canvas

Devil's Nightgown is probably a forgery. Fox, a minor but influential fixture of the 1970s art world, was extremely prolific, and for a time her paintings fetched ludicrously high prices, so much so that in the late 1970s and early 1980s, a forger known as Lieutenant Furlington created over one hundred Fox imitations, which he quickly sold to collectors eager for their own Foxes. After his arrest, Furlington admitted to faking *Devil's Nightgown*, and Fox herself has no recollection of painting it, yet here it stays, attributed to Fox nonetheless because it is a very good Fox.

The leaves of the devil's nightgown discharge a semitoxic secretion known for its encephalitic properties. In the seventeenth century, Puritans used the devil's nightgown to treat lethargy and hubris by burying the afflicted for three days in a womb of the enormous leaves of the plant. During cold New England winters, children still use the leaves as sleds, and in the Pacific Northwest, where *Archegonium mathildis* is rare, fur trappers gnaw on the acerbic leaves and use the roots as currency.

Kornelia Werfel

American, 1953–1995

Muskrat or Beaver #3, 1983

Oil on canvas

Werfel painted a series of close-ups of both beavers and muskrats, challenging viewers to answer the eternal question, "muskrat or beaver?" *Muskrat or Beaver #3* is an optical illusion—seen one way, the face of a muskrat becomes clear, but seen another way, the face of the beaver emerges. Who can say how one differs from the other? They are both creatures of the night and water, lost souls swimming toward the horizon of distant memories, as fleet in their milieu as a moth is flitting through air. If you listen carefully to the faint whisper of their twitching whiskers cleaving the aquatic surface, you will hear your new commands.

The muskrat is the beaver of my mind; I'll soon be with you, my love.

I'll soon be with you.

Eternity is a long time; so is life—the notion that she will join the husband who preceded her in death terrifies her. Perhaps he should be the one who is scared—to be rejoined by the woman who prayed so hard for him to die until it worked. She watched him go. You have been repaid, she thought. You and all the husbands of the world: the violent, the distant, the corrupt and debased.

Can an afterlife be her reward? Reuniting with her mate is no heaven. Maybe it is the fear of an afterlife that has kept her alive for so long.

I'll soon be with you, my love.

Aaron Gill
American, 1905–2010

Marmot Island, 1985
Found objects, taxidermy

Need I describe what you can easily see with your own eyes?

Jasmine Burns
American, 1958–1999

Closed Road, 1990
Oil on canvas

The canvas is thirty-six inches wide and twenty-four inches tall. Beginning in the upper left corner of the canvas, one can see the blue of the sky through diaphanous clouds, a mixture of black, gray, another kind of black, and two whites with an almost undetectable amount of pewter. In the middle of the painting is a lot of sky. To the right of the sky is more sky. Moving down, on the left side of the painting, to the right of the tree, is sky.

Midway down the canvas, below the tree, one can see a greenish field—a lot of green, a bit of yellow. To the right of the field is more field, and then a gray road that extends inward toward the middle background, disappearing into the mountains. We are meant to feel loneliness when we see the road that nobody would want to travel on. We feel lonely because it is a lonely road. The road makes us grateful for our inadequate homes and families. We yearn for the warmth of shelter when we see this road. To the right of the road is a dead and brittle field with a single tree that almost blends into the bleakness. To the right of the tree is an old, strangely colored horse [gray, olive green] looking for food in the dead field. The color of the horse suggests that a child painted it. The horse is hungry and thirsty—all the food has died and the water dried up. The horse will be dead soon too, its body left alone in the field to be consumed by bald eagles and flies. To the right of the horse is more dead field and to the right of the dead field is still more field, also dead. On the lower right side of the painting is the artist's signature, vivid blue. It is a large, bold signature, even for Burns, and is the most vibrant element of the painting. Our eyes are drawn here, to the corner, to this bright artifact, as if the artist's boredom in painting this lackluster landscape was worth it because, at the end of the day, she could sign it, sell it, and get it out of her studio.

Roscoe Crooks (born Matthew Peuse)
American, 1930–2005

Good-Looking Horses, 1985
Oil on canvas.

Good-Looking Horses depicts the aftermath of the notorious Horse Massacre of 1875, in which sixty-four broncos were decapitated and burned to combat an outbreak of equine vampirism near Thermopolis, Wyoming.

Collectable figurines inspired by *Good-Looking Horses* are available in the gift shop.

Iris Babbitt

American, 1940–2007

Night Storm, 2005

Latex house paint on plywood

I find Babbitt's residue on the wooden floors of the upstairs hallway, kneel, and draw lines through the spectral dust. When I see her standing in my bedroom doorway, her body is nearly opaque, though her face is like the water of a pond that has been disturbed and muddied by something escaping to deeper waters. Her liquid features are a smudged copy of Babbitt in life—I can see her eyes, her quivering lips, open as if to say something. She opens her arms, and though I am tempted to run toward her, I know I will only pass through her. Her skin and the robes that shroud her fade like a photograph left in the sun, and she becomes a blur of color. I yearn for the real Babbitt; this poor, empty copy—this afterimage—is no longer enough.

Artist Unknown

The Labyrinth, ~1920s
Dollhouse from the Kendall Seagrave Memorial Dollhouse Collection
Gift of the Ambrose J. and Vivian T. Seagrave Family Trust

Although not technically a dollhouse, *The Labyrinth* is doll-sized, and here dolls roam the maze while the Minotaur, unknown to them, lurks at the center, ready to devour those who lose their way. Kendall Seagrave disliked the labyrinth, perhaps because of the monster at its center, or perhaps because whoever created the system of stone walls neglected to include an entrance or exit. The particular terror of dropping a doll into a labyrinth-without-escape was overshadowed by the need of the Minotaur to eat, so Kendall sacrificed three dolls to it each week, choosing the oldest and most ragged ones, dolls who were perhaps ready to die anyway.

Every painting a miniature, a window to some unknowable place with an unknowable past. Frames like the covers of a novel. Every life a glimpse.

She is alone, and she has always been alone—her past now only figments.

Perhaps here on this bench she will allow herself to die. She will gather the light around her again, allow what was forgotten to stay forgotten, focus on the feeling of her body, her breath, inhale the stiff, artificial air of the gallery, savor the feeling of what it is to be alive, pray for darkness, and exhale.

ACKNOWLEDGMENTS

Endless thanks to Susan McCarty for her enthusiasm, editorial guidance, for visiting countless museums, and for being my partner in crime. This book is for Susan and Mattie, who fill me with love and wonder every day.

Thanks to Mom and Dad for their love and support. Thanks to Aaron Burch, Russ Brakefield, Craig Dworkin, Hilary Plum, Zach Savich, and Barrett Watten for their varied and meaningful advice, encouragement, and friendship. Thanks, as always, to Karen Brennan, François Camoin, Melanie Rae Thon, and Lance Olsen for all they've taught me.

Thanks to the best colleagues in the world for their love and support—Christine Hume, Carla Harryman, and Rob Halpern.

Thanks to Nicola Mason for taking a chance and for all her hard work making this book as good as it could possibly be. Thanks to Barbara Bourgoyne and everybody at Acre.

Thank you to Eastern Michigan University for providing time and financial support in researching and writing this manuscript.

Thanks to the Art Institute of Chicago, where the idea for this book was born, and to the many museums whose exhibit labels provided valuable guidance and inspiration—The Detroit Institute of Art, The Met, MOMA, The Guggenheim, Dia:Beacon, The Museum of Contemporary Art Chicago, The Met Breuer, The Hirshhorn, The National Museum of Art, The Phillips Collection, The Whitney, Palais de Tokyo, the Louis Vuitton Foundation, the Norton Simon Museum, and everywhere art is celebrated.

Thanks to the editors of *DREGINALD* and *Puerto del Sol*, who published early excerpts from the manuscript.

